MAGICAL MIDLIFE FLOWERS

MAGICAL MIDLIFE FLOWERS

K.F. BREENE

ONE

"G MINUS SEVERAL SECONDS, JESSIE," Edgar said as he poked his head into my small sitting room at the back of the house. He reached in a spindly finger. "G minus several seconds. Sound the alarm. The all-clear commences tomorrow."

He issued a thumbs up, nodded, and slowly disappeared from the doorway.

Austin, sitting beside me on the couch with his arm around me, stared at the doorway silently for a long moment. I waited patiently, holding back laughter at the bewilderment tumbling through our bonds.

"What?" he finally asked. Then, "Wait...do I want to know?"

The laughter finally bubbled out. "This is Nessa's doing. She said 'T minus eight minutes' the other day.

Edgar decided it was a great way to do a countdown, except he muddled it badly and kept changing letters, then the numbers were wrong too—he just went completely off the rails. Nessa thought that was hilarious, and has been teaching him other stuff."

"The all-clear commences tomorrow?"

"He doesn't seem to understand the things she's teaching him. I'm just letting them roll with it. It's like their own secret code where neither party has the decoder ring."

He shook his head, taking a deep breath. "This place is like a circus."

"Yeah. With drunk clowns. It keeps things interesting."

"So...what is he actually counting down to?"

I leaned forward to grab my phone. "The flower exhibit, remember? He's been working all week to set up his entry at the Martin County Fair."

"Ah." He nodded, squeezing me closer as I leaned back. "That's tomorrow, right?"

"Yep," I replied. "He hasn't allowed anyone to see his design. He's going to unveil it to us tomorrow morning, right before the judging. They're going to keep the exhibits up for the entire week of the fair, I guess, so it should keep him out of the way while we get ready to head to Kingsley's territory. You know he's probably not going to want to leave his flowers."

"Who'd you decide to bring as security?"

I wouldn't really need security, especially with the whole house crew there, but we had a bunch of new gargoyle guardians in the territory, and Austin wanted to take them out for a test drive. Not to mention they were accustomed to escorting their cairn leader everywhere and wouldn't understand if I didn't bring any of them.

"Tristan, of course." I'd only known him for a short time, and already he seemed like the most competent choice. "He's picking a team of five."

"Only five?"

"I mean...yeah. We're going to a non-magical town for a flower show. We'll have ten people from the house, including me, and two additional mages. Adding another six hardcore guardians will be plenty. More than plenty. We're going to stand out."

"Not the new healer?"

A healer had arrived not long ago, responding to a summons I'd sent out after the battle in the basajaunak lands. She was staying on the outskirts of O'Briens, getting a feeling for what she'd randomly and apparently thoughtlessly walked into. I was giving her time and space before we figured out if she was a good fit, although her lack of planning definitely suggested she might be one of us.

"Nah. We don't need to expose her to Edgar's flower obsession so soon," I said.

He stroked his thumb against the bare skin on my arm. "I'm part of the house. Don't I get to go?"

I pulled away to look at his face. "Do you *want* to go?"

A handsome smirk flitted across his lips. "Not even

remotely, no. But I do want to see who Tristan chooses and how he handles the guardians."

"He's been exceptional in training. I can't imagine this would be much different."

It had only been two weeks since Tristan and the other new guardians had joined our ranks, and already they fit like cogs in a well-oiled machine. Part of that was Austin's infallible leadership and natural ability to structure a large pack, but Tristan had helped the other guardians acclimate.

With all of our new additions, our territory was currently bursting at the seams. We'd already put out feelers to purchase land to build more housing.

"He has, yes," Austin said, sipping a bourbon. "I want to see how he handles chaos, though. Outside of training, your crew always descends into chaos."

I rolled my eyes but couldn't come up with a rebuttal. He wasn't wrong.

My phone buzzed with an alert, and I distractedly clicked through to social media.

"What did you have—" Austin paused as I sucked in a startled breath. "What is it?"

"Nothing," I said, scanning the image that had popped up.

He leaned over my shoulder to see what had my attention. For some reason I couldn't really understand, I jerked the phone away from his prying eyes.

A woman smiled up at the camera, joy written plainly across her pretty face and lighting up her brown eyes. She held up her hand, showing off her new diamond solitaire. The caption said, "She said yes!" and Matt, my ex, was smiling for the camera next to her. Although she and I weren't connected online, he was tagged in the post.

This was the woman he'd left me for. A decade younger, it looked like, with flawless tanned skin and shiny straight black hair. Her smile was so big, teeth pristine and white. Her eyes were so happy.

Something heavy lodged in my gut, and my heart started beating a little too quickly.

"Are you okay?" Austin asked me, concern and confusion muddling the bonds.

"Yeah, I'm fine."

Unable to help it, I clicked into her profile and started scrolling through photos of the new life they shared, with a big house and brand new cars. I hadn't kept up with him since our breakup, much too busy and not really caring, but now it hit me like a Mack truck. He clearly took her out to fancy dinners and theater shows. He'd lost a little weight and dyed his thinning hair black to look a little younger than his mid-forties. To keep up with her, probably. Or maybe because of a midlife crisis, who knew.

It had barely been a year, and he was moving on. For good.

I'd already moved on, of course, but I guess I hadn't fully processed the end of an era. The feeling of the book slamming shut on part of my life story. I felt... strangely panicked, like I needed to lurch forward and rip the book back open. I had no idea why.

Then I wondered if he'd told our son, or if Jimmy would find out the same way.

In a moment I'd tapped Jimmy's name on the screen of my phone. I could feel Austin watching me, but he didn't try to interfere.

"Hello?" Jimmy answered.

"Hey, it's me."

"Hi Mom. What's up?"

"Did you hear about your dad? I just saw what I gather is an engagement photo."

"Yeah." Jimmy couldn't have sounded more bored if he'd tried. "He said he'd be asking her to marry him when I visited last spring."

"Did he ask you for permission or just tell you?"

"Why would he ask me for permission?" Jimmy asked, confused.

"I don't know...in case you didn't like her, maybe?"

"Nah, she's fine. Just a little too nice or something, I don't know. She tries way too hard. It's weird."

"She's young," I said, trying to be nonchalant about that. For some reason I couldn't explain, it galled that he'd essentially traded me in for a younger model.

"I mean...she's not that young. Why? You don't care, do you? Aren't you still with your boyfriend?"

"Yeah, yes, I am. It just...feels so sudden, I don't know. It's kind of a shock."

"Well, Mom, I mean...he was always going to find someone else, you know that, right?"

I paused. "What do you mean?"

"He doesn't cook or clean or do anything for

himself. All he does is work. That's all he ever did. So obviously he was going to find someone to do that for him when you two separated. He probably knew he had to seal the deal with her quickly or risk her leaving. And anyway, you've moved on, too. You have Austin, right? I like him a lot. You're a lot happier now. I doubt it'll be long before he pops the question to you, so it's not like you've been left high and dry or anything, right?"

"He won't pop the question, no. That's not really... how shifters work. But...yeah, you're right." I sighed, shaking my head. "I was just blindsided, is all. I just ran across a picture on social media."

"Trust me, Mom, you've got a way better setup than he does. You have that huge house, the butler, a boyfriend who does all the nice little things you like, and magic—I mean, now you have *magic*, Mom. Don't worry about Dad's deal. You're much better off as you are, and he's going to be exactly the same as he ever was. Win-win for both, right?"

"Right. Definitely."

When had I started needing pep talks from my son instead of the other way around? I laughed at the absurdity of it all—my reaction, the reality check from my son, and the fact that I cared at all about the man I'd moved on from when I had the catch of the century right next to me.

"Anyway," I said. "The beat goes on."

"Oh-kay. I gotta go, though. You sure you're good?"

"Yes. Thanks for parenting your mother, Jimmy," I said with a laugh. "Are you still coming for Christmas?"

"Yeah, definitely. I'll probably have to visit Dad for a couple days. He is already trying to schedule everything—you know how he gets. But I'll spend most of my time with you, if that's okay?"

"Of course! I'd be thrilled."

"Okay, gotta go. I'll call tomorrow. Bye."

"Bye," I said, but he'd already severed the connection. I sighed and placed the phone on the coffee table before sitting back. Only then did I notice how still Austin was, his demeanor solemn.

Confusion and then alarm bled into me. How must this mild freak-out have looked to him?

"I'm sorry," I said quickly, hugging him from the side and leaning my cheek against his shoulder. "I really don't care, honestly. I was just blindsided, as I said to Jimmy. I knew Matt would get married again, it was just weird putting a face to the situation. And she's younger and super pretty and..." I shrugged. "It makes no sense, I know, but—"

"You have nothing to be sorry for," he replied, rubbing my arm. "It makes perfect sense. Do you need some time? Should I give you space to sort your feelings out?"

"What? No! Not at all." I hugged him a little tighter. "I don't even know why it struck me. Or why seeing her face, all happy like that, would annoy me. There's no logical reason for it. I wish it would just stop."

"What has happened?" Mr. Tom pushed his way into the room, his tux a little rumpled from being worn all day. "Has Austin Steele said or done something to affect you, miss?"

"No, it's nothing, Mr. Tom. My ex is getting re-married—"

"Oh." Mr. Tom clasped his hands in front of him and tilted his head to the side in sympathy. "I see. You need a postmortem." He nodded, coming farther into the room. "Well, we have a week or so before we leave for Kingsley's, and your past lover is not far away. We can fly there tomorrow and pop in on them. It would get us out of having to go to Edgar's ridiculous flower contest."

"No, I don't need a postmortem. It's nothing, honest."

But I couldn't banish the memory of their smiling faces, and the sinking feeling in my gut wouldn't relent. She wasn't *that* much younger, for heaven's sake! Plus, she was going to age and I wouldn't. She'd catch up eventually. There was no need for this situation to trigger my insecurity. It was irrational.

"But seriously," I said, still annoyed, glancing from Mr. Tom to Austin and then back, "since when did he let his significant other post pictures about their life together? He never let me do any of that."

Was it because he'd been embarrassed of me, the way he'd always implied? I hadn't come from a high-class family, or gone to private school before college (or even finished college because Matt wanted to start a family), or had nannies and horse-riding lessons. Maybe this new girl was everything he'd wanted me to be.

After another deep breath, I waved it away. "Maybe it's just me being competitive, I don't know. He's all happy and smiling and on social media, and I haven't said a peep to him about how happy I am." I leaned into Austin, needing him to know my happiness was, in a large part, because of him. "Or that I've moved on to someone *way* better. I mean...I guess I'd like him to know that just because he initiated the split doesn't mean I'm hanging on or anything."

"You should post those things, Miss," Mr. Tom said. "Let him see how happy you are."

"I should. And what's the deal with him taking her out all the time?" I clicked back into the app and flicked through her pictures, not able to help myself, now somewhat spiraling. "He hardly ever took me out. We always had to entertain his mom or his co-workers, and *I* had to cook and set up and do everything. Theater? Fat chance. He always said he hated the theater. His idea of going out was to have a couple of drinks at the cigar room after work with his buddies while I waited at home alone." I crossed my arms over my chest. "When Jimmy visited him, he made it sound like it was the same ol' Matt. Well, my Matt never took smiley pictures with me on nights out."

"He might not have in the end, miss," Mr. Tom said, "but I bet he did in the beginning, hmm?"

Austin just sat next to me silently, showing his support by listening, his arm draped around me.

I narrowed my eyes at Mr. Tom, thinking back. But it had been so long ago and we'd been so young. My memory was splotchy at best, the details long since washed away. All I remembered was how handsome and dashing he'd been, well-off and always nicely dressed. He'd had a nice car—an expensive car—and I'd been stunned by his attention to me. What we lacked in common I'd made up for by trying to learn his interests and appeal to him. So we hadn't started on a good foundation, and with time, that foundation had crumbled.

"Regardless," Mr. Tom said, "I think this is an easy problem to rectify." He lifted his eyebrows. "We will invite him and his whole family for Thanksgiving or Christmas, and you can then shove your happiness in his face. That will be nice, won't it?"

"His mom traditionally has a party the day after Christmas but no." I furrowed my brow at him. "I'm not going to be petty. Honestly, let's just forget about it. I'll come to my senses any minute and go back to not caring. It's fine."

"If you say so, miss. Should I get you a glass of wine? Or something stronger? Maybe you'd like to dwell a little over a pint. The horrible Irishwoman is in her backyard drinking the basajaunak brew and singing like some sort of dying wild animal. She could be a distraction for you."

"I'm good, Mr. Tom. Thanks."

"Of course, miss. Let me know if you need

anything, like a plan to out-happy your ex." He exited the room and closed the door behind him.

I ran my hand up Austin's thigh, smiling as he squeezed me closer.

"Sorry," I repeated, snuggling into him. "I didn't realize he could still throw me for a loop."

"I understand how you feel, Jess," and I could feel through our bonds that he did. He kissed my forehead. "When my first girlfriend moved on, I had some rage issues. I knew she was bad for me, but it still set me off. Some of these things hold onto us without us realizing. That's why I offered to give you some space and let you deal with it."

"And here I was worrying you might feel slighted or nervous that I still have feelings for my ex."

"It would only be a matter of time before you came to your senses. I have zero fear of losing you to anyone else. Our bond is unshakable. Your heart is mine, and mine is yours. But I will admit it's a little awkward dealing with an ex that I can't just force into submission and make go away."

"Well I mean...you *could*. I doubt it would be hard. It just wouldn't be nice."

He pushed up and angled before capturing my lips. Heat coursed through my body.

"I'll meet him one day," he murmured against my lips. "And when I do, I'll make sure we shove our happiness in his face right before I prove how nice I most certainly am *not*."

TWO

JESSIE

"Wow." Nessa eyed me as I came down the stairs. "You have a helluva glow about you today. Special occasion last night?"

"Another bang-a-thon," Ulric said as he passed me and then her, heading for the door. His hair stuck out in all directions. "Sometimes her ability to heal is not ideal. If they get tired from all the banging, she can just heal him up for another round."

"I didn't heal him at all last night," I replied haughtily. "I did it this morning because he had to get up early to check out a disturbance on the territory perimeter. Some foreign shifters are testing our defenses, I guess. He only just got back." I could sense him outside, waiting with the rest of my people. "I wouldn't want to send my man off to work tired after all the work he did for me last night."

"It is truly a shame that female gargoyles are so rare," Ulric muttered as he headed out the door. "Truly a shame."

It *had* been a marathon last night. Austin had been staking his claim, ensuring I knew what I had with him. I'd risen to the occasion, wanting to prove my devotion and apologize for my temporary lack of rationality. I couldn't have been any more secure in our relationship today than if there'd been only one man in the entire world and I had him. Which might as well be the case. There was only one man for *me*, at any rate, and after forty years on this earth, I'd finally found him.

Besides, Jimmy had been right. I had magic now! A lot of it, with all the perks of this house to go with it. I'd leveled up into a dream life (except for the danger, which I would currently ignore so that I could comfortably gloat). My ex might've started out a few pegs above me on the social hierarchy ladder in the Dick and Jane world (and his family and friends had made sure to constantly remind me of that), but I was part of a different social hierarchy now, and he couldn't hold a candle to my position. Suck it, Matt.

Just for good measure, though...

"Nessa," I said as I met her at the bottom of the stairs. "Do you or Sebastian know much about social status in the Dick and Jane world?"

"Obviously. Mages make a habit of dominating Dick and Jane social tiers so they have access to rich and influential people. That leads to an in with politics, and *that* leads to the creation of laws and bills and legislation that will help their organizations prosper. We don't dabble much in that arena but we certainly know the players and the rules. Why do you ask?"

"My ex just got engaged, and I—"

"Oh man. That's annoying. How are you coping?"

I paused, then shrugged. "I had a minor freak out yesterday, but I'm good. It was just weird seeing his fiancée out of the blue like that." I explained what had happened.

"Who left who?" she asked as we stepped out onto the porch.

"He technically left me, but I was ready for a change. More than ready."

"And he left you for this current woman?"

"Yeah. Apparently he met her through work."

She scowled. "That's so lame. He found a replacement before he even broke it off? I'd want to stab him, I think. That'd piss me off."

"Honestly, I didn't care. I *don't* care," I amended. "His news was just a shock, that's all. I'm over it."

"I bet she's younger, too," Nessa mused.

I hesitated. "Uh...yeah. Yes, she is. Pretty, as well."

"That's so cliché. With big boobs?"

"I...don't recall."

She nodded solemnly. "He left first, he moved on first, and now he's doing *forever*..."

"Technically I did 'forever' first, though," I hastened to say. "It just doesn't translate to the Dick and Jane world because shifters do things differently. I didn't rub it in his face, though." I hesitated again and then braced my hands on my hips. "Which...fine, he hasn't rubbed it in my face. I happened upon a picture. But I also didn't splash my happiness all over social media for him to find. He never posts, but he posted a couple pics of them together."

I'd broken down and checked last night out of curiosity. Then I'd gotten annoyed again since he'd never done that with any of our stuff. He never posted about Jimmy ever. Yet here he was, posting about her.

"This is dumb," I said quickly. "I don't care about this. Forget I mentioned it."

"Why didn't you post your happiness on social media?" Nessa asked me, ignoring what I'd just said.

I watched Edgar shove Jasper into a haphazard sort of line with the others.

"Honestly, because Matt never allowed me to put our personal stuff on social media, and I got in the habit of looking but never posting. He always used to say it was an invasion of privacy and invited gossip."

"Yet he's now posting, and so is she?"

"He only posted those couple of pictures. Maybe he hasn't put the foot down with her, I don't know. Or maybe..." I felt the twinge of an old pain. "Maybe he's not embarrassed by her the way he sometimes was about me. I didn't fit into his world as well as I probably should've."

"Ew." She made a sour face at me. "I'm going to pretend I didn't hear that last bit while simultaneously planning his destruction. Does the fiancée post about just their happiness...or their happiness *and* their life?"

I frowned at her. "What?"

"Does she post about mundane stuff? Here, lemme see." She grabbed the phone out of my back pocket, shoved it in front of my face to unlock it, and started peppering me with questions on how to find his fiancée's account. In a moment, she was biting her lip and nodding thoughtfully. "Yeah. Oh yeah. Hmm."

"What? What is it?" I asked, drawn in despite myself.

"He never *allowed* you to post, huh? He called the shots?"

"Kinda. I mean..." I winced. "He just got—"

She put up a hand. "No, no. I gotcha." She surveyed me with narrowed eyes, and I got the feeling my entire existence was being picked apart and studied. In a moment she nodded to herself, resuming her perusal of the photos. "I don't think I fully understood your history. Yeah, this woman is almost solely posting about what a wonderfully happy couple they are and how their life is so great. It's like her world revolves around him."

"That's kinda how it goes with him. I can't even explain how he does it, but before you know it, he's your whole world and you don't have any friends or anyone who's close to you anymore but him."

She lowered the phone slightly, sliding a glance my way.

"Anyway." I reached for the phone, but not before

Nessa took a snapshot of the screen and sent it to herself in a text. "It doesn't matter. I've got an amazing life here. I'm good. I need to let it go."

"Nope. No way. He's *allowing* his woman to only post happy couple pictures. He is obviously advertising how great his life is now that he's moved on. Or how great he's made her life now that he's in it. It's warfare, and we won't stand for it. You're about to blow up his feed, baby girl. Leave it to me. You'll come out on top."

I grimaced as I watched her walk off the porch with determination. *What've I done?*

"Miss Jessie." Edgar, who'd been studying everyone like a drill sergeant, stopped at the bottom of the porch steps and looked up at me. His hands twisted around each other as he brought them up to his chest. He looked like some old vaudeville villain. "I don't want to alarm you, but we are at fox-tango-eighteen."

His grimace could make the unsuspecting faint with his large yellowed canines, the tips stained darker as though he'd just been feeding.

"Right. Of course." I checked the time. We needed to get loaded up. "Shall I get everyone going?"

His sigh was cute. "Yes, please, Miss Jessie. Thank you. Thank you! *Thank you—*"

"Back in line," I barked at him, both to give the moment a little occasion and to stop him from carrying on.

He scurried across the grass and I surveyed my crew.

Then sighed.

How in the hell was Nessa going to make this outfit look glamorous?

AUSTIN

AUSTIN STOOD on the edge of the grass, out of the way, surveying Jess's crew. They stood in a haphazard line on the sidewalk outside of Ivy House, chatting and joking like a bunch of school kids waiting to go into class. Cyra stood at the head of the group, randomly swinging her arms.

Tristan waited about five feet away from Cyra, wearing a black button-up shirt and trendy jeans, not as dressed down as Jess and her crew usually went for. His hair, kept a little long, loosely curled around his ears with a stray curl draping down the side of his forehead. A five o'clock shadow covered his chin, and his shoes weren't freshly polished to a high shine.

Usually he'd have his guardians waiting in a crisp line beside him, matching the discipline of Austin's shifters. There were no shifters today, though, this situation totally and completely under Jess's supervision, and the five guardians next to Tristan waited in a haphazard line.

He'd read the room.

The guy was clearly a chameleon. Austin had heard about his past, mostly that it was a potentially dangerous mystery. Tristan must've had to get good at fitting in so no one would question his origins. It served him incredibly well here.

Austin made his way to the head of the Ivy House line. "You missed the mark," he said conversationally as he stopped beside Cyra.

"What?" Cyra stopped waving her arms and looked down at herself. "I'm wearing underwear this time! And socks!"

"I don't think he was talking to you," Hollace murmured.

"He couldn't be. I even ironed! I am ready to play support system...even though I'm not exactly sure what that means."

"It's what they call going to a flower show," Jasper grumbled, "when you'd rather have needles stuck under your fingernails."

"They can both be arranged, if you'd like," Edgar told him pleasantly, entirely serious. "We can do both at the same time if that would make you more comfortable?"

"Just go back to counting," Jasper replied.

"Good idea. C minus one minute, everyone!" Edgar called. "I am so excited for you to see what I've done! You're going to *love* it."

"I never wear underwear," Dave said, puffing up in pride. "I can pee anytime, anywhere."

"We can all do that," Ulric replied.

"How so?" Tristan asked Austin, correctly assuming that *missing the mark* comment had been for him. Austin was grateful for the distraction from the others' conversation.

"Your dress code is too formal," he said.

Tristan looked down at himself. "Turns out they don't sell threadbare jeans in your shops. Surprising, since all the shifters seem to own a pair." He was poking fun, something almost no one did with Austin, given his position. This gargoyle had balls. Austin liked that about him. "I usually dress to the nines when on a detail like this, so I figured this was a good middle ground instead of going for a sleeveless shirt or a lumberjack flannel."

"I would've voted for the sleeveless shirt," Nessa said as she sauntered by. "Ya got nice guns."

"Find me later," he replied. "I'll strip down and show you what else I've got that you might like."

"Fat chance, loser," she quipped, flashing a smile as she passed Edgar and gave him a thumbs up. She stopped next to Sebastian, removed from the line on the grass.

Tristan maintained his smile, watching her.

"I don't speak for Jess," Austin said when Tristan's focus returned to him, "but I doubt she'd care if you dressed more formally."

"Maybe we should all dress more formally." Cyra looked around Austin to see Tristan. "He's very handsome. I think we'd all look a little more handsome if we dressed better."

"We do dress a little better usually," Jasper said. "When we're not going to a *flower show*."

"Okay, okay." Jess put out her hands to calm everyone down. "Let's all get on the same page." She looked pointedly at Jasper. "We're just waiting for Mr. Tom to do...whatever it is he is doing, and we'll get underway. What's the transportation situation looking like, Tristan? Who's driving what?"

She looked over the assortment of vehicles waiting behind them. There were a couple of sporty cars, one of which was the Porsche Jess had gotten as a gift, a few town cars, and a couple of vans. He'd assembled enough transportation to carry a party three times the size of the group gathered in front of Ivy House.

"The guardians will drive, miss," he told her, his wings fluttering.

"Great. Which...ah..." She let the words linger, used to having Austin or Mr. Tom arrange the menial details, knowing she took joy from not having to deal with it herself.

Austin hadn't mentioned that to Tristan. He also didn't help navigate the situation now. He wanted to see if Tristan could acclimate to her easygoing personality after being with a regimented leader for the last fifteen years.

"There are more cars than guardians," she finally said. "Who's driving the rest?"

Tristan's wings fluttered again, a gargoyle's way of advertising their acceptance of a command or engagement in a conversation. That's what he'd been told, anyway. In Austin's opinion, it was essentially movement for movement's sake, intended to draw attention to their wings, especially those with a larger set. The habit annoyed the shifters, but Austin wasn't going to put a stop to it until he learned more about the layers of meaning.

"We can take whichever cars you would prefer, miss," Tristan responded with a small bow.

Her brow furrowed. "Oh, I don't care. Edgar, this is your thing. You can choose."

Tristan's wings stilled now, her delegation apparently throwing him for a loop.

"What a treat." Edgar beamed, turning around to survey the vehicles. He started mumbling a pros and cons list to himself.

"Should I interject?" Tristan asked Austin in a murmur.

"Too late," he replied. "Now you just have to ride whatever comes of it."

"In battle and in training, she takes a firm leadership role. I know she's easygoing, but I didn't expect her to hand off the reins entirely."

Austin allowed himself to chuckle. Gargoyles didn't take exhibits of emotion as a weakness or reason for a challenge. To them, a predator was just as dangerous when smiling as when not wearing any expression at all. There had been a lot of shifter/guardian challenges before the other shifters had learned that lesson.

"It's not handing over the reins, it's letting someone else choose the transportation. She is a very laid-back person, yes, and she lived with a controlling man for half her life. She doesn't sweat the small stuff. She's used to letting someone else handle it. To keep control of the situation, I organize the environment and let her handle her crew. I've always said that I am the castle to her keep. You'd do best to think of it like that."

He nodded slowly as the banter around them died down, ending with Cyra offering to demonstrate the best way to pee in the woods using her current body. Before meeting her, he'd had no idea phoenixes changed bodies like a Sims player changed skins.

"Here we go, here we go!" Mr. Tom zoomed out of the front door carrying a large basket. "I have coffee for everyone. Except for you, Dave. For you, I have a lovely herbal tea I've made from magical flowers. It tastes absolutely wretched to me, but I am sure you will love it. I have plenty of breakfast sandwiches and burritos—oh." Mr. Tom stopped at the bottom step, looking at the guardians. "No shifters. Why did I assume there would be shifters?"

"I don't know, but you made an ass out of you and me." Jasper grinned. Then elbowed Ulric. "Get it? Because *ass-u-med?*"

"Well, never mind." Mr. Tom continued down the steps. "I'm sure the guardians are plenty hungry. I have one more basket to bring out and then we are ready."

"D minus—"

"Edgar, honestly," Mr. Tom berated, stopping at the bottom of the porch steps. "Stop with that. One wonders if you can actually tell time. Why are there so many vehicles? Are there more people coming that I can't see? I might need more coffee—"

"Okay, okay!" Jess clapped and walked forward. "Edgar, we need that decision. It's time to go."

"Yes, Miss Jessie." Edgar loped toward the sporty cars. "I think I had better ride in the Porsche with Trident—"

"He means you," Cyra told Tristan. "He's bad at names. And thinking."

"—since I am the orchestrator of the flowers. I think you and Auntie Steele would be most comfortable in one of the black cars, don't you? And the rest can file into the vans."

"Let's all just take the Town Cars, shall we?" Mr. Tom headed to the second in line. "I think that would be best." He popped the trunk and put in the basket before opening the lid. "Miss, you and Austin Steele will be in the first car, of course. Or would you prefer to be in the last?"

"Whatever," she said, starting forward.

"Fantastic, first it is. Edgar, no, get away from there. We've only just employed that guardian, we don't need to scare him off so soon. Tristan, you can drive the miss. Would you like a coffee for the road? I didn't make one of your exciting creations this time. You'll have to make do with creamer and sugar."

"I'm..." Tristan shook himself out of a stupor. "I don't need coffee, Mr. Tom. Thanks."

"Let's go, now. Let's go." Mr. Tom started shepherding people toward the cars. "No, no coolers," he scolded Niamh. "Leave that blasted thing behind."

"Ah sure, I might as well take it," Niamh drawled, not giving it up.

"Word of advice," Austin said to Tristan before joining Jess, unable to help himself. He tuned the argument between Niamh and Mr. Tom out. "It might be better to call her in advance to see what she wants or if she'd prefer for you to make the arrangements. When in doubt, be decisive and direct your crew to get moving. She'll follow suit and they with her. That way, you won't get upstaged by an old as dirt butler."

"Noted," Tristan growled, directing his people to get moving.

"Sir, here you go." Mr. Tom handed Austin something wrapped in foil. "Egg, cheese, extra bacon. Miss— oh, she's already in the car."

Austin got into the car beside Jess.

"I see now why you always like to bring some shifters," she said once the door was closed.

"Why is that?" he asked, entwining his fingers with hers.

"Because that way you can control everything around us and calm down my crew's craziness."

He smiled, watching as Tristan found his way to the driver's side door and stood there for a moment, monitoring everyone. Guardians re-organized the extra vehicles they'd brought, moving them out of the way.

"Yes, a tip I just gave Tristan. Be decisive so that Jess doesn't have to."

She leaned into him. "Maybe that's a bad thing. Nessa just reminded me that I basically let my ex control me. He called the shots—most of them, anyway—and my voice was lost. I shouldn't bring that into my new life."

He shook his head as Tristan opened the door. "I don't know about your situation in the past, but you always step up when you need to. It's not a bad thing to be easygoing, Jess. If you don't care about the details, there's no reason you should feel the need to throw your weight around to control them. You have new people now. They'll adapt to your style. This is probably the best way to practice. What could possibly go wrong at a flower show?"

THREE

Jessie

"Miss!"

We'd barely finished parking and Tristan had just turned to tell us something when Mr. Tom started knocking on my car window.

"Miss!"

Tristan gave a bewildered look at Austin.

Austin, in a move that was odd for him around a subordinate, even in my presence, started laughing.

"Don't get out yet," Austin told me. "Just roll down the window. I need a word with Tristan."

I did as he said and Mr. Tom leaned in toward me. "Miss, do you need a refill on your coffee?"

"No, thanks, I'm fine."

"And what about a bite to eat? Now, I know you weren't hungry enough for a whole breakfast sandwich or burrito before we left, but it's been nearly an hour. I packed plenty."

"I ate before we left, Mr. Tom. I'm good."

"Yes, miss. But what about a muffin? Or a croissant? Or a chocolate croissant?"

"No, thanks, Mr.—" I paused. "A chocolate croissant might be nice. And I guess just a bit more coffee with it. Just creamer. No sugar."

"Fantastic, miss. Chocolate always hits the spot in the morning. How about you, sir? I see the wadded up foil. Would you like another?"

"No, Mr. Tom," Austin told him in a commanding tone. "That'll be all. Deliver Jess's food and give us a moment."

"Yes, sir. Tristan? Do you need to put in a quick order before I am thrust from the car by the alpha's command?"

"No. I'm good," Tristan replied in a deep voice brooking no argument.

"Very well." Mr. Tom hurried from the car.

Tristan's strangely glowing eyes flashed in the rearview mirror. "Is that a usual occurrence when on the road? I don't remember him being this...overbearing over the last couple of weeks."

"There was a plane ride lacking snacks at one point," I said with a smile, "and he's been a little...much ever since. You'll get used to it."

"You probably won't," Austin said and I mock-frowned at him.

"Here we go, miss." Mr. Tom was back, handing

over a little plate with a croissant and a fresh travel mug. Once I'd taken it, he handed in a napkin and hurried off, calling out offers of food to the others.

I rolled the window back up.

"Should I give you guys a sec?" I asked. Tristan's frown was clearly visible in the rearview. "What?"

He shook his head a little, glancing at Austin and then away. "I beg your pardon, miss—"

"You don't have to be so formal with me, Tristan. I'm not from a long line of alphas like Austin."

"Right." He rubbed his chin, a scratchy sound. "Sorry, it's just...I've never heard a leader ask if he or she should remove themselves from a meeting of minds. Usually they do everything they can to listen in."

"I trust my people," I said simply. "Even the sneaky ones, like Niamh. I trust them to do what is in my best interest, and they trust me to do everything I can to make sure they're taken care of. Most of all, I trust Austin. If he wants a heart-to-heart with you and it would be better for him to do it without me here, that's fine by me."

"What she really means is, can she be excused so she can eat her second breakfast." Austin ran his hand along my thigh, smiling at me. "Tuck in, Jess. Save me a bite, though."

"I'm going to tell Mr. Tom you're having second thoughts about more food."

"How dare you," he joked, taking up the saying Mr. Tom had grown fond of lately. Then he leaned back, looking at Tristan. "I was going to take a spectator role on this one to see if you could figure things out, but it seems like you're reeling. Should I step in?"

Tristan considered the offer in silence. I appreciated his willingness to give it real thought. It meant he wasn't the type of guy to give false assurances or back down immediately when things got rocky.

I couldn't fathom what was so hard about accompanying my team, though. They were chatty and disorganized, sure, but they weren't completely crazy. Not usually. And as Austin had said, it was just a flower show. A flower show in a mostly non-magical county. The plan was to show up, have a look around, wait for the judges to make their ruling, and leave. Sebastian and Nessa had assured us the mages would be tucked away, gearing up for the battle with Kingsley, and we had a large team with us. What was the big fuss?

"I'll keep my position as point," Tristan finally said. "It's a good exercise. Would you mind…Jessie, if I spoke to Nathanial about the crew? It might be nice to get a little more input from someone who doesn't know you as well as Austin Steele."

"Sure," I said through a full mouth, flakes of croissant stuck to my cheeks. I offered him a thumbs up before I took a sip of coffee. Once I'd washed the bite down and wiped my face, Austin grabbed the pastry for a bite. "Feel free to make yourself at home with them," I added to Tristan. "With us. Ask questions, hang around the house, whatever you need."

He nodded, studying me in the rearview mirror for a second. Maybe to determine if I was serious. Apparently realizing I was, he nodded a second time and looked away.

Austin handed back the croissant he'd taken more than one bite of and reached for my coffee.

"How *dare* you," I told him, allowing him to take it anyway.

Tristan reached for the croissant next.

I pulled it away. "We're not *that* friendly."

He laughed and faced front again. "We're not chocolate-sharing friends yet, got it."

"While you're both here." Austin sobered. Tristan immediately did as well. I finished the croissant as Edgar loomed near our car, peering in the windows with an anxious expression.

"We need to get going," I murmured.

He nodded. "The territory breach this morning was fairly well organized. They've been happening more often of late, shifters all. I'm not sure yet, but I'm getting the feeling it's the same pack. The style of attack is too eerily similar for it to be various packs. It's nothing we can't handle, but if the breaches get any bigger, or they don't start tapering off, I'll be using your crew, Jess, and the guardians, Tristan, to make a statement. I want this place quiet when we leave. That might take a little bloodshed."

"Send the basajaunak after them." I wiped my fingers on the napkins. "They'd be more than happy to handle the situation in a spectacular fashion."

"They aren't technically part of your crew, right, Jessie?" Tristan asked, still trying to make sense of everything. He was using too much logic, that was the problem.

"They are and they're not." I toggled my hand back and forth. "Dave is solidly on my crew. The others have made a trade with me—they can live in my wood in exchange for protecting my territory. I don't use commands with them, though. Except maybe not to kill anyone. I want them to feel at home, because that makes it more likely they'll want to protect that home. Besides, if you get too pushy, they are liable to take offense, and then they might try to snatch off your head and kick it around. Literally. But ultimately, they have not made any sort of alliance with us. I think it would take their lead basandere to do that."

Austin moved to get out of the car and Tristan followed quickly, opening my door for me.

"I see," he murmured, keeping pace with me as I headed over to Edgar.

"Ready, Miss Jessie? Uncle Austin?" Edgar practically bounced from one foot to the other in excited anticipation.

"Uncle?" Ulric asked with a wide smile. He started laughing, and Nessa slapped a hand over her mouth to keep from joining in. She elbowed Sebastian, who shook his head, not wanting to get involved.

"Ready," I replied with a laugh, slipping my hand into Austin's. His bewilderment rang through the bonds.

"The gates don't officially open for...some amount of time," Edgar said, heading to a side gate. "But I wanted to show you my display before the judging."

"An hour, Edgar," Mr. Tom said. "Honestly, *do* you know how to tell time?"

"Since when has he needed ta, like?" Niamh asked. "He just farts around the garden all day until we tell him to head into battle."

"It's a peaceful existence," Edgar said pleasantly. "Until battle, of course. And then it is heart-clutchingly scary."

Nessa glanced at Sebastian with a gleeful smile, reveling in Edgar's oddness.

"I really shouldn't be bringing this many people," Edgar continued, mostly just muttering to himself now, it seemed. "I told them I was inviting the queen, though, and she would need her bodyguards. And also my sisters and brothers from the house. K-list celebrities are not to be sneezed at, I told them. It would bring honor to all the lands."

"K-list?" Ulric glanced back at Nessa with raised eyebrows. "Honor to the lands? You're getting a little out of hand."

She bent over laughing as she walked. Niamh, who loved playing jokes on Edgar, laughed alongside her.

"After a while they relented," Edgar continued, apparently not noticing the chatter around him.

We approached the side gate. A heavyset guy in a bright construction vest sat on a metal folding chair with a walkie-talkie.

He looked at our group in mild disinterest, his head already starting to shake, before he caught sight of Dave in the middle. It wasn't hard. He topped our heights by several feet, had a hairy head and body, and wore a kilt he'd possibly borrowed from Phil, Niamh's basajaun drinking buddy. The man's eyes widened and his mouth dropped open.

"We need that potion, Sabby," Nessa said immediately, digging through the crossbody bag resting on Sebastian's chest. "I told Dave they'd notice him, but he didn't believe me."

"Yes," Dave replied as Nessa pulled out a little vial and pushed through the crowd to get to him. "This Dick seems very observant."

Austin braced himself, about to step forward, but hesitated. He'd clearly meant what he'd said about letting Tristan take point.

Thankfully Tristan recognized it and pushed through the group, stopping in front of the stunned guard as Nessa lifted the vial up, trying to feed it to Dave.

"I have it," Dave said, gingerly taking it from her with his massive hand.

"What's the hold-up?" Tristan demanded, and everyone looked his way with suddenly tense bodies. Something in his tone suggested nightmares not yet realized, unspeakable horrors about to unfold. The cadence of his speech—and the dangerous intent behind it—seemed to lazily curl through the air, slithering along my skin and making me shiver. It didn't seep in, though. It felt like it could crawl along my bones and splice into my muscles, but it didn't, instead leaving a strange haunting residue in its wake.

"Well, I'll be," Niamh murmured softly, her eyes slightly narrowing.

"What is it?" I whispered as Austin took one step forward, half blocking me from Tristan even though we were a few paces away.

"It's another clue, is what it is," Sebastian muttered, taking a step closer and moving his fingers. Meanwhile, the potion kicked in and Dave disappeared from sight. "Another facet of his type of magic."

Tristan glanced back at Dave, and I knew he could see him. The magic Niamh was talking about was blood magic, and in addition to whatever it was he'd just done, it also helped shield him from mage magic. Or, in this case, helped him see through invisibility potions.

Tristan nodded and took a step back, bending quickly to grab the walkie-talkie falling from suddenly loose fingers.

"Niamh," Tristan said, a command riding his words.

She somehow knew what was expected of her.

"Let us through, there's a good lad," she told the guard, taking the walkie-talkie from Tristan and handing it back to the guard.

"But..." The guard blinked, his gaze now rooted to Tristan. His brow furrowed with confusion. He glanced at the crowd of people, probably looking for the

Bigfoot he could swear he'd seen, but came up empty. Instead, he latched onto the next oddity. "Why are they all wearing capes?"

It was Nessa's turn now. Bounding up with a laugh and a smile, she touched the guard's shoulder and glanced her leg against his thigh. "We're here for the flower exhibit, of course. It wouldn't be any fun if we couldn't do a little cosplay with it, now would it?"

She batted her eyes at him, always smiling, and Tristan laid his hand on Edgar's shoulder and pushed him through the gate. He grabbed Cyra next, ushering her through.

"Let's go," he urged in a low tone.

The others caught on quickly, slipping past the bamboozled guard and into the fairgrounds. Austin and I were last, Austin's bearing and gaze hostile, pounding his menace into the guard.

"We good?" he asked, and the other man wilted under his dominating presence.

"Y-yes, sir," he said immediately.

Austin nodded, and then we were through as well, the guard staring after us with his hand clutched to his chest.

"Is anyone going to ask what that feeling was?" Ulric raised his hand, looking around.

"No," Niamh replied. "Yer knowledge of what Tristan can do does *not* leave this group. Do ye hear me?" She turned and speared Ulric with a stare. "We will simply be glad ta'have one more tool in our kit."

Ulric put up both hands now. "Yeah, fine. I won't

cause any trouble for him. I was just curious. Does it get any more potent, or is it just a general feeling of... not nice?"

"It was not directed at you," Tristan said, falling back. Edgar remained in the lead as though nothing at all had just happened. Flowers were the only things on his mind. "You only got the backsplash. I can't stop that from happening."

"And so the target gets...what, exactly?" Sebastian asked, sticking close to Tristan.

"Ye have some sort of death wish, so ye do," Niamh muttered at Sebastian.

"No, just a passion for magic and all its intricacies," Sebastian replied.

"The target experiences varying degrees of a nightmare," Tristan said. "I went easy on the guard. For others, I can crank up the power and trap them in their own personal hell."

"Huh." Sebastian nodded. "Jessie has a spell like that. Interesting. Do the effects linger?"

"The target will feel shaky and rattled, but once the magic is pulled away, the nightmare dissipates entirely."

"And you're fine with them knowing?" I waggled my finger through the air, indicating the guardians within hearing distance.

"They're aware that my origin is unknown," Tristan replied as we turned down an empty thoroughfare. To the sides, vendors were setting up their stands or food trucks, getting ready for the fair to open. More than a few stopped and watched us walk past, their eyes invariably finding Tristan or Austin. "They know it didn't affect my status in my old cairn. Everything else is just noise."

"Everything else is just..." Sebastian looked around Jasper, walking beside him, to peer at a guardian. "You can do magic—potent, potentially devastating magic—and they shrug it off?"

"Not everyone is as inquisitive as you are," Tristan replied.

"Not everyone..." Sebastian scratched his head. "I have no words."

"That's good, because here we are." Edgar stopped in front of a domed building, its roof reaching about two stories high, with dark tinted glass doors currently closed. An awning spanned over the entranceway. Even though the interior was dedicated to flowers, the ground outside was plain concrete.

"This is the first time I have entered a contest," Edgar said, "where we needed to create an overall aesthetic. It's not just about the quality of the flowers this time, which I of course excel at—"

"If ye call cheating excelling, sure," Niamh mumbled.

"—it's about the overall *design* of the exhibit."

"Oh no," Jasper said softly.

Edgar took a sweeping bow. "I think *some* of you will especially like it." He beamed at the gargoyles in turn. "I dedicated it to your kind."

"Oh *no*," Jasper repeated, a little louder.

Niamh had started to quietly chuckle, and Nessa gave her a suspicious side-eye.

"Oh no," it was my turn to say.

I had a feeling Niamh had played some sort of hand in Edgar's design, and knowing her jokes on him, it would likely be a spectacle in the very worst of ways.

FOUR

Jessie

The perfume of a crapload of flowers in a closed environment assaulted my senses. With trepidation, still holding Austin's hand, I walked down the wide pathway between two exhibits. One was a play on *Alice In Wonderland* and the other some sort of fairy forest setup with little fairy doors, toadstools, and moss. Both attractions had water features designed to look like natural streams, with the flowers organized around the accessories in a pleasing way. I found myself pausing now and again, actually quite liking both setups.

"Yes, yes, take it all in," Edgar said, his hands behind his back, feigning patience. "I'd hate it if you solely experienced mine. There are some fantastic efforts through here. What do you think, Ulric?"

"Uhhm," Ulric said softly. "The Mad Hatter's tea party is cool, I guess."

It was the area with the least amount of flowers.

The next couple of attractions also had pretty cool themes, one with a *Men in Black* situation and the other fashioned after a Japanese-style garden. I perused them slowly and Austin kept pace. He slipped his arm around me, tucking his hand into my back pocket.

"Are you bored?" I asked him, moving on to the next one.

"Not at all. It's nice. I've never been to a flower show."

Near the wall, I stopped as I reached a display without a discernible theme. "Oh wow, look at this one."

I curled my arm up and lightly grabbed the bit of shirt over his heart, leaning against his side and taking it in. A little stone archway embedded with a metal gate and surrounded by flowers reminded me of one of the hobbit holes in *Lord of the Rings*. A similar archway was filled with wine bottles, the bottoms facing out, toward the audience. Water streamed around them in the middle, pouring into a little pond at the bottom, encased in vines. A few new pennies sparkled within the shallow water, and I knew they were encouraging people to make a wish. The flowers were vibrant, all different colors, but organized in such a way that they didn't feel too busy.

"This would be a cool backyard," Jasper said,

standing beside me. "Look at the wine barrel waterfall up top."

He pointed to a cool water effect that tumbled down from a grouping of barrels and stone, the water gathering into a little canal that disappeared behind the flowers.

"This artist might be someone we invite out to the winery to bid on the landscaping job," Austin murmured, leaning down to kiss my temple.

"Keep your voice down," I whispered. "If Edgar ever found out I hired out for that, he'll go ahead and retire himself. He won't wait for me to do it for him."

Austin laughed as we walked on, not taking my comment as seriously as he should have.

"Mimi should see this," he said. "Why didn't she come? She's initiated herself as part of your house crew, I believe."

Austin's grandma had decided she'd be more useful to our territory than to her own. She would officially move to O'Briens after Kingsley's pack was secured. Her plan was to stay at Ivy House, as she'd already been doing, until she found a place of her own. None of this had been discussed with me. I'd merely been informed and told that if she became a nuisance, I could just kick her out. As if I'd ever do that.

Given she still had so much work to do on Ivy House, and we would have huge builds in our future to accommodate our growing pack-slash-crew, I was relieved she was staying. She would be a great help, not only for that, but also because she seemed to understand and agree with my style of management.

I'd ended the one-sided conversation by shrugging and telling her to clear it with Austin. According to him, he hadn't gotten a chance to argue, either, but I knew he was happy to be strong-armed into the arrangement.

"She said she had better things to do than waste time looking at amateur flower growers." I stopped at the next exhibit, not as taken with their house of cards theme. "It's too bad she's not here, though. Some of these are really great. She could have helped us steer Edgar in a different direction."

"And Patty?"

"She has something planned with a woman in town or something. I think she was thinking along the lines Naomi was."

"Hey, pretty couple, look this way!"

I glanced over at Nessa, who had her phone held up to snap a picture.

She lowered it again and winked at us. "That was a good candid take. It shows you weren't posing for the other one I just got, which is totally adorable and going to make everyone jealous of what you two have."

"What is she talking about?" Austin asked as Nessa bounded away, meeting Sebastian at a different exhibit.

I shrugged. "We chatted about the whole ex thing earlier."

"And?" he prompted.

I shrugged again.

"Jess?" He slowed, pulling me a little closer. "What about the ex thing?"

I quickly led him through our earlier conversation as we hit a wall of flowers—a literal wall with flowers emerging from the cracks or hanging from rings embedded in stone. Moss was glued onto rocks at the bottom, and a few areas were wet, as though the fabricator had attempted a pond or stream or something and missed the mark.

We turned the corner as I finished, feeling strangely competitive about the whole thing. Like I didn't want to let Matt have the last say. I had a good life now, dang it. I wanted to make him a little jealous. Sue me.

Austin stopped and turned me before threading a piece of loose hair behind my ear.

"I guarantee they don't have a love like ours, Jacinta Ironheart," he said softly, his breath fluttering my eyelashes. "Our love has been building all our lives, waiting for the day we found each other. I know his fiancée situation is very fresh, and it's bringing up a lot of old animosity, but soon it'll fade into the background and you'll realize you care less now than you ever have."

"I know that. I do."

"And in the meantime, I will of course help populate your social media with pictures to drive home the point that you are *mine*. No one else, certainly not your ex, can hope to find a connection as deep and meaningful as what we share. If you want, I'll help make your ex feel insignificant in comparison."

My heart surged, and my hands tightened around his neck, dragging his lips down to me. I held on tight, wishing we were alone. I needed to do something for him, to show him what he meant to me. To appreciate him. A date, maybe. A perfect date, like he'd once taken me on, but this time it would be all the things *he* loved.

He broke the kiss, holding his lips inches from mine, and growled, "And about him controlling you... don't think for one moment that was your fault. He took advantage of you when you were too young to push back. Maybe when you didn't know you *should* push back. Or could. But the woman I met, before the magic, was no pushover. She's even less so now. You've learned your lesson, Jess, and now you're with a man who would never take advantage of your kind soul and easygoing nature. You're safe with me. Be the person you want to be, unapologetically, and only allow those who appreciate you into your life."

I ran my thumb across the bare skin of his neck. "You always build me up."

"We support each other to achieve our best selves."

I nodded, kissing him again. "You're a rare sort of perfect, Austin Steele. I'm the luckiest woman alive."

He smiled. "I'm only perfect for you. To everyone else, I'm a nightmare."

AUSTIN

AUSTIN LOOKED DOWN at the woman of his dreams, hating the hurt she felt at rehashing her past. Because that's all this was. He'd done something similar with his old girlfriend Destiny—theirs had been a love gone wrong, twisted and vile, but it had been love all the same. Losing it had made him reflect on the person he'd been and the person he wanted to be.

She'd get past this quickly, he had no doubt. He liked the idea of collecting pictures, though. Of sharing their life with friends and family. He'd nailed down his forever, and he wanted his family and her son to share in that.

"Isn't it perfect?" Edgar asked down the way.

"*Ohhhhhh noooooo,*" Jasper said from the same location.

"Jessie," Ulric called in an urgent tone. "You should come see this."

She kissed him again before tearing herself away, turning and hurrying after the others. Whatever Edgar had done promised to be cringe-worthy, Austin had no doubt. He watched her go, taking in her shapely butt.

"Best pic yet." Nessa waggled her phone at him. She'd hung back too. "What do you think about the whole ex situation, Mr. Protective Alpha?"

He started forward slowly, wanting Jess to get a chance to do damage control before he stepped into whatever mess Edgar had concocted. Too much of their crazy was bad for the senses.

"We all have them," he replied. "Sometimes it's not fun dealing with them."

"This is true. But you do intend to help her?"

"Of course."

"Of course." She tossed up her hands like she should've known his answer. "You'd do anything for her."

"Yes."

"Like maybe...stop thinking like a shifter and think like a Jane for a moment?"

He frowned down at her. "How so?"

"You're mated, right?"

He didn't answer, waiting for her to get to the point.

She nodded like he'd given a verbal answer. "But have you had the fancy shifter mating ritual dinner thingy? I mean, sure, she stayed in your house for a while, but you didn't have a big celebration."

"We haven't had time."

"Living together? You don't. Not really. Sharing of assets? How can you when you don't live together?"

"We have the winery—"

"That's not done yet."

"—and we'll have some big builds coming up—"

"You're still talking about the distant future. Look, alpha—may I call you Austin just this once?" She put her hand on his forearm, her comical approach easing the sting of her words. He knew that was on purpose.

"Austin, you've claimed each other. That's a big deal in shifter land. It's sacrosanct. But in Jane land, and mage land, and most other lands, my girl's got nothing to show for what she has with you. She's got nothing to brag about. I mean, sure, soon she'll have pictures, and you're a looker, so that'll go far, but to non-shifters, you're just her boyfriend. A boyfriend she loves very much, but as everyone knows, boyfriends come and boyfriends go."

He stared down at her, frustrated because he knew she was right.

She removed her hand before holding it up in a stop motion. "I know that you haven't had two seconds to rub together since the mating happened. I'm not faulting you for how things currently stand. And I'm not suggesting you rush into a mating...dinner or whatever it is. Instead, you should think about how Janes do things, and maybe incorporate some of that into your plan going forward."

"Like marriage," he said.

She toggled her hand. "Maybe not marriage per se, but a proposal would certainly go a long way. A really nice one in a special place with a ring and a photo opp. I'm not gonna give you details. I hear you're romantic, so you can think of something." She made a fist. "Give my girl bragging rights so she has some ammo when she talks to that idiot ex of hers. I bet he's the type to lord things over people. We need something robust to knock him off his pedestal."

He shook his head, mystified. "You've known about

all of this for...an hour? Two? You sound like you already have a plan for putting her on top of a social situation completely peripheral to all the other stuff we have going on."

"An hour was plenty of time to sort this out, are you kidding? I could do this in my sleep. My girl is annoyed. She basically wants peace and joy for everyone, so this guy must be a next-level asshole for her to feel anything less for him. She needs people on her side, and I'm going to be the arsenal he never saw coming."

She lifted her fist into the air.

"I'll do those things," he finally said, "but not to rub it in her ex's face. I'll do them because I love her and want her to be happy."

"Yeah, yeah. Sure, sure. Just do them sometime this century, maybe. That's all that I'm saying. And wear a nice outfit and take a picture or two." She gave him a one-shoulder shrug. "No biggie. Say, where's that hot gorilla you usually have hanging around? Why didn't he come to this here shindig?"

"You have a masterful way of dancing around potentially explosive topics."

"I do, don't I? I've had a lot of practice. Now, about that gorilla...?"

He huffed out a laugh, shaking his head and starting toward what must be the exhibit. She passed him, not something he'd let just anyone do, and walked a little in front.

"I'm not sure. I don't check in when he's off duty. Maybe you should?"

She smiled over her shoulder at him. "Are you playing matchmaker, alpha?"

He didn't respond, only willing to get involved so far. Brochan was a troubled man. He needed more people around him. More friends. More fun. The problem was, he wouldn't allow himself any fun. He needed someone to draw him out, but as the alpha, Austin wasn't in a position to do that. Brochan needed a friend on his level or outside of the pack. Hopefully Nessa or even Tristan would rise to the occasion.

She laughed at his silence, easing the mood.

Tristan's presence lurked just in front of her, his gargoyle magic helping him blend into the wall of the pavilion. She slammed into him, her expression turning surprised and her hands reaching up to stave off the unexpected roadblock. He became visible immediately, turning to find her flailing within his wings.

"You need to move, *daddy*," she said, and it was clear she was trying to taunt him in some way.

"I don't take orders from you, little monster. But keep stroking those wings, and I will certainly move." His tone dripped with innuendo and Austin stepped to the side to pass them.

"I'm not interested in that sort of movement," she said, pushing against his arm to move him herself. Given their difference in size and muscle mass, Austin wasn't sure why she'd bothered.

"Are you sure?" he said softly, and Austin noticed the goosebumps spreading across Nessa's exposed skin.

It was clear that she might not want to be affected by him, but that didn't stop it from happening.

Tangled webs. He didn't envy them that dance. He was happy to be on the other side of it.

It took him a few moments to reach the others, and then no time at all to stop dead and wrestle with the impulse to let his mouth completely drop open.

What in the holy hell?

FIVE

Jessie

I HADN'T STOPPED STARING since I'd first set eyes on it.

There were no words.

None.

Well...except for batshit crazy. Those were a couple of words that might work for Edgar and this situation.

"What in the beejeebus?" Jasper asked, sounding like he was out of breath. "What. In. The. Holy. *Beejeebus?*"

"The horrible old woman is responsible for this, I know full well," Mr. Tom said indignantly. "No way would Edgar have created this...this..."

"Triumph?" Edgar asked with a beaming smile, standing in front of his creation, tucked in the back corner of the pavilion. I wondered if that was by choice, luck, or the mercy of the establishment. "Heartfelt homage to the great gargoyle?" He turned and pointed. "Look! I even used that little figurine Jessie got as a conduction gift."

"Connection request gift, I think he means," Ulric said, spotting the little statue at the same time as the rest of us. It was the little gargoyle with stained glass wings that had so repulsed Mr. Tom.

"Yes." Edgar put his hands behind his back. "Niamh said it was a great favorite."

"I knew you were behind this." Mr. Tom pointed at her, standing on the other side of our crew.

"What's the fun of a practical joke if ye can't make it a *big* one." Niamh grinned...and then smiled...and then started to cackle.

"Horrible," Mr. Tom sputtered. "Absolutely horrendous. I've never seen such a degrading display! A slight to our kind. A stick in our eye!"

"I don't think that little...statue thing is the real issue here," Ulric said.

"That is definitely not the real issue here!" Jasper said loudly, his fists balled. "I can actually *feel* the crazy emanating off this exhibit. Miss Jessie..." He turned to me, his eyes wild, shaking his head. "I can't... This is... I can't..." He closed his eyes, still shaking his head.

Niamh laughed harder, now echoed by Nessa.

"What's the matter?" Edgar asked, imploring Mr. Tom. "Is this not the statue of the gargoyle god?"

Niamh doubled over at that. The guardians looked between each other and then at Tristan, who was standing back a ways, surveying everything with an uncustomary blank face except for some tightening around his eyes.

"Dang it, Niamh," I grumbled. "If you scare Tristan off, I will never forgive you."

"He had to be indoctrinated eventually," she replied. "Might as well get it over with. There's no way to escape it."

Naomi had mentioned that Edgar was making a shrine using another statue we'd been gifted as a connection request—a kinda misshapen male figure— and here was the proof.

It stood in the middle of Edgar's elaborate setup like a welcoming sentry. The head and face were covered in pink and white roses for hair, and it had a huge flower beard almost down to its chest. Daisies covered the eyes and some sort of ivy sash entwined with flowers draped over its chest. A string of tulips circled the waist and a grouping of sunflowers covered its junk like a cloth. The base was completely covered in flowers, and more grew in the ground just beneath it. Under the sash of ivy, bright red painted lines outlined the misshapen and twisted abs, two dots representing anatomically incorrect nipples.

A shallow pond glimmered in front of the statue, reflecting the light from overhead so it splashed across the statue and danced across the flowers. Stone pillars rose up at various heights, each of them displaying the kind of store-bought stone gargoyle used to scare people at Halloween. Ivy crawled up the cylinders, giving the display a nice pop of green. The stained-glass gargoyle was displayed in the uppermost corner, as though perched on an old church and readying to fly.

I hated to say it, because of how he'd worked that statue in the middle, but the actual layout was pretty good. There was a discernible pattern, unlike at Ivy House, and the colors worked with each other nicely. It made me wonder if the overkill at Ivy House was solely due to Edgar's flower overproduction for the basajaunak. I struggled to remember what it had looked like before Dave.

"I felt an actual shrine would've been too much," Edgar was saying, admiring his creation. "I mean, they didn't give Jessie a shrine, did they? They merely gave her the god statue. So that gave me the idea of a natural light reflector pool and the offerings of flowers and decorations you see here."

"Jessie, I hate to say this," Ulric whispered, pushing in close, "because the vampire has his uses and he's sweet in his own way, but maybe you should re-think your stance on retiring him."

"And now, for the special part." Edgar turned back with a sly grin. "No accusing me of cheating this year. These are not specially formulated flowers. I was going to use those, but Sebastian's elixir made them too large. They simply wouldn't do. I made these using my old recipe, and they worked out much nicer."

I glanced at Austin in confusion, only then realizing he'd started to back away again, pointedly leaving this situation to me and/or Tristan.

"But...isn't that old recipe also magical?" I asked.

"No, no." Edgar waved that thought away. "That was just the local witch who helped me with that. Nessa says witches aren't the same as mages. Since Dicks and Janes can also be witches, it stands to reason that witches shouldn't be considered magical. So my old recipe is on the straight and narrow. It's perfectly fine."

I was pretty sure a great many of us were blinking rapidly, trying to make sense of that logic.

"I don't know much about magic," Tristan said into the din, his voice unusually harsh, "but I've never heard of flowers that follow a conversation."

"I'm afraid to ask what he means," Jasper whispered to no one in particular.

"The flowers in the back are moving," Tristan said. "The two sunflower-looking things. They keep moving their...flower heads. Like they're listening to the conversation. There's no wind. Their stalks and leaves shouldn't be swishing and swaying, especially because they're not doing it in sync."

"Ah." Edgar put up his hands in triumph. "Yes! I almost forgot. Miss Jessie, I must say, I have outdone myself on this one. I have finally perfected the magical attack flowers—"

"Didn't he *just* get done saying that he didn't use magic?" Ulric asked Jasper.

"Oh no." Edgar waved at Ulric. "Yes, I see the confusion. No, those particular flowers have been a long-running experiment resulting in a great many cuts and near-death experiences. I think I've finally nailed the art of the attack flower, though. You see, these are as docile as you please to friends, and incredibly violent to foes. I included them just for their appearance. Their magical properties have nothing to do with their visage. It still counts as normal."

"Cheat to win, aye?" Niamh drawled, wiping tears from her eyes.

"How does it know friend from foe?" I asked, trying to reserve judgement for the time being.

"They imprint on those who spend time with them while they are growing up. Good singing, bad singing— telling it stories!—all of it will help the flower imprint on its new friends. The basajaunak are just in love with them. Ask Dave. Oops. We can't. He's invisible and muted. You'll have to take my word for it. These flowers make great listening buddies, too, as my friend Tristan has realized."

"Uh-oh, Sabby," Nessa murmured. "He's replacing you as his bestie."

"I'm really okay with that," Sebastian whispered.

"I'm not," Tristan responded wearily.

"Okay, wait." I put out a hand. Forget judgement, I was diving headfirst into panic. "Wait a minute. Let's forget for a moment that you are incorporating *very obviously* magical flowers into a non-magical flower show and focus on this friends vs foes situation. Are you telling me these flowers might attack anyone they don't know?"

My crew waited in silence for his answer. Other

voices started to float through the space, either judges or the creators of the other exhibits. We had precious little time to figure this out.

"Technically...yes," Edgar said slowly. "But don't worry, I asked to be way in the back here, and they are stationary flowers, as you see. They will not grow legs and run after anyone. Not yet, at least. I'd hoped to speak with Sebastian about that for the next generation of flower—"

"But...Edgar"—my voice was rising in pitch—"there is a path right next to that one attack flower. And what if a kid gets loose and tramps over to that gargoyle by the other flower? You can't have these flowers attacking people. Attack flowers are incredibly vicious."

"I see the concern, but rest assured, there are only two of them, and I will be here the entire time. I will not move, day or night, as I watch over the people of this county and my precious homage to the great gargoyle."

"I'm touched and repulsed and a little freaked out, all at the same time," Jasper whispered.

"Yes," Mr. Tom said, "he has that effect on people. Miss, if I may, we'll want to be wrapping this up. I hear people slowly trickling this way."

"Edgar..." I stared at him for a silent beat. "Edgar," I repeated in a deeper voice, finding I was really at a loss for words this time. I felt like saying his name really ought to be enough. "I think I'm going to have to restrict your time in non-magical areas if you can't see the problem with playing sentinel twenty-four/seven at a county fair. Regardless of the fact that they won't let you stay here after hours." I held up my hand to stop his rebuttal. "Sneaking around the fairgrounds at night and sitting in here in the dark is not the answer to this problem. That's the way you scare people half mad. Now, we need to get those flowers out of your exhibit."

Edgar wilted. "Yes, Miss Jessie."

The flowers' movements were subtle. But now that they had my attention, I could see them moving and swaying like Tristan had said. It was like they were programmed to softly dance in the breeze, but each responded to a different one. And yes, their large flower heads, like sunflowers, did move. They seemed both intelligent and responsive to sound.

To say it was unnerving was putting it mildly. They should be relegated to Ivy House soil and nowhere else. They were much too creepy to co-exist with normal people.

"But Jessie..." Edgar slowly raised one spindly finger. "There's just one problem."

"And what is that, Edgar?" I asked, pushing through everyone to get to the easiest-to-reach flower.

Tristan stepped forward immediately, right at my back. Austin did the same, probably wanting to be close in case something went wrong.

"I can't just rip them out."

"Yes, you can, Edgar," I said firmly. "You have to. You cannot have magical flowers—flowers that move and *follow conversations*—in a non-magical place, and you can't have *attack flowers* anywhere, except maybe at home."

Laughter rang out from somewhere in the pavilion. More voices drifted toward us.

"No, Jessie, you misunderstood me. I physically can't rip them out. They have magically fortified stalks, so they are hard to cut down, and their roots are essentially one big anchor. They are incredibly tough to eradicate. I didn't want them easily hacked down the next time Ivy House is under attack."

"Yet you planted them *here?*" I screeched, panic rising.

"Well, you see, they were in a pot. It was a good, sturdy pot made of—"

"Get to the point," I barked as the nearest flower watched me approach. It stopped swaying, standing dead still now, and something about that made me shiver.

"Well...they somehow broke through the pot, burrowed into the concrete below, and I assume into the earth below that? I figured the conundrum of removing them could wait until the fair is over. They really are a lovely addition to the aesthetic as a whole, and quite unique. I essentially bred this flower myself. It's a cross between—"

"Edgar," I snapped to shut him up. I was about at wit's end.

"Is this real life?" one of the guardians asked Jasper.

"Bro..." Jasper shook his head. That was all the

answer he could give, it seemed. I got where he was coming from.

"What's our play?" Tristan asked me gruffly.

"Good question," I murmured, stepping closer to the thing.

Its leaves started shaking, and a gap opened up in its flower face, revealing what looked like fangs made out of thorns.

"You have got to be kidding me," I groaned.

"Careful, Jessie, their thorns are poisonous," Edgar advised. "Here."

He hurried to get in front of me, putting up his hands for the angry flower, which topped my height by about half a foot.

"Now, now," Edgar told it. It didn't have eyes, but I could swear it was still watching me over his shoulder. "She is *friend*."

It opened its flower mouth wider and issued a hiss. Little droplets of liquid fell from each of the thorn-fangs. Leaves straightened from its sides and then curved like hands, and I noticed little spines on the edges that looked capable of cutting and ripping skin. It bent in our direction aggressively, and it was clear it would go through Edgar to get to Tristan and me.

Just about everyone backed up a step, including Tristan's guardians, their wings fluttering and uncertainty on their faces.

Tristan, however, didn't balk. He stepped forward, putting his arm in front of me, intending to shepherd me back to safety.

"No." I used magic to help shove him away. "You're much too green to be dealing with something like this."

These weren't gnomes we were dealing with, and Ivy House couldn't step in if needed. This was magic gone rogue in a place with unsuspecting civilians. The most dangerous kind of situation.

What could go wrong at a flower show, indeed.

SIX

"Sebastian," I barked, making everyone flinch. "Give me the revealing potion or give Dave the anti-serum. We need to see and hear him. Dave, join us, please."

"He's right behind me," Tristan said. "He says to step aside. He'll handle this."

"She is friend," Edgar told the flower, putting his hands up to it again. "*Friend.*"

"Does anyone have a machete?" I asked, stepping to the side just a bit and motioning for Tristan to get out of the way. "Sebastian, I need that revealing potion."

"Here, Jessie, I've got it." Nessa handed me a vial. "I just gave one to Austin as well."

In a moment, Dave was revealed to me, his hair all puffed out and his palms up as he and the flower stared each other down.

"They can see through invisible potions?" I asked in dismay.

"Yes, of course," Edgar told me, his hands still up. He looked at me over his shoulder. "Well...sense more than see. We couldn't have people sneaking past them with something as simple as a potion. That would defeat the purpose of a watch flower."

The flower leaned forward, fast as lightning. The petals surrounding its face slashed through Edgar's skin, slicing his shirt and opening a gash.

"Ow!" Edgar jumped back. "You naughty thing! That hurt. Now, now. Calm down. These are *friends*." He waved at me. "Don't worry, Jessie. It's just a flesh wound. When the flowers get testy, they lash out. They don't mean any harm." He paused for a moment. "Most of the time."

"What do we do, Miss Jessie?" Nathanial asked, always quiet until needed. He stepped over the exhibit line and into the space between the red rope and the non-lethal flowers.

"Oh, careful there, Nathanial," Edgar warned. "You're in the danger zone."

More voices filtered through, closer now.

"Dave, you grapple with that thing," I told him, stepping in front of Edgar. Tristan picked the vampire up and pivoted, depositing him out of the way.

"Mind the flowers of the exhibit," Edgar called.

I sighed. "Yes, try not to hurt Edgar's non-lethal flowers."

"Jessie, this is not the time to be supportive of his flower hobby," Jasper said in bewilderment.

"We'll do what we can," I replied. "Okay, I'll use magic to saw at the base. Once we get this one, we'll *carefully* get the other one. Hurry now, and watch out for that poison. Edgar, how fast will it kill?"

"Not for at least an hour, Jessie. It'll just hurt before then. You'll have plenty of time to heal Dave if something goes wrong."

"This whole thing is wrong," I grumbled, getting to the rope fence with my hands out.

The flower faced us, looking between Dave and me with feral intelligence.

"I have taken down magical flowers before, Jessie," Dave said. "I know what to do."

"Well...those were a little less hardy," Edgar told us. "They had fewer organic weapons. What you're looking at here are Attack Flowers 3.0. They really are quite revolutionary."

"And they're at a county fair," Ulric said dryly. "We should've brought my mom. She would've beaten it into submission by now."

He was probably right.

"Dave, you cover that side of her, and I'll cover this one," Tristan said, moving into position. "Poison doesn't affect me as quickly as most."

"I can help," Cyra said. "I'll burn it."

"You'd end up burning the whole exhibit down," I told her.

"Very probably," she replied. "Would that be a bad thing?"

"No," Jasper responded without hesitation.

"That wounds my soul a little," Edgar murmured.

The flower shook wildly now, its leaves fluttering, its stalk jiggling, and its head moving so aggressively I was surprised all the petals didn't fly off.

"Here we go," I said, my heart hammering.

It launched toward me, somehow sensing I was the ringleader. Dave grabbed it before it could reach me, getting sliced by a leaf that sent blood dripping from his hand down its stalk. Tristan grabbed its head, wrenching it toward him. His grunt said something had impaled him and it hurt.

I dodged a leaf, felt the slice of another, and exploded into my gargoyle form to keep from taking harsher damage. My clothes tore away from me. Another leaf hit my tougher gargoyle hide, barely breaking through. I called up magic quickly, using a harsh spell to hack at the stalk. That spell would've sawn an arm in half, but it barely caused a surface wound.

"Think it through," I heard Sebastian say from somewhere behind me. That was his anthem for when a dangerous and perplexing problem presented itself to him. "Think it through."

I tried another spell as Dave and Tristan fought the flower, Tristan trying to rip its head off and Dave tearing at a leaf. This spell sliced a little deeper, and the flower screeched—a high-pitched sound that Edgar must've borrowed from the Ivy House dolls. I shivered in disgust. I didn't need any more nightmares resulting from that house.

Sebastian rattled off a couple of spells for me to try at maximum power. He waded into the fray, shoving Tristan to the flower's opposite side so he could bend down with me. He stepped gingerly despite hurrying, careful of the non-lethal flowers, supportive of the team to the last. He was a keeper.

I put out an arm, blocking a leaf from stabbing Sebastian.

"Thanks," Sebastian said distractedly, hanging back behind me a little as I took the cuts and scrapes and continued to saw at the thing with magic.

Dave ripped off another leaf before roaring, and I was suddenly glad we'd left him invisible and muted. The whole pavilion would've heard that.

My previous slice began to heal. A new leaf sprouted where Dave had ripped the other off.

What was this thing, a bionic flower? What the hell had Edgar mixed together to create it? I'd've been impressed if it weren't giving us such a hard time.

I stepped back, power welling, angry now. Supporting Edgar be damned, I'd smite this whole exhibit if I had to.

"Wait, wait..." Sebastian grabbed my arm to stop me from unleashing a spell. "Wait, I have an idea. Call them off. I think we can go a different route."

I took a step back as Dave punched the flower in the proverbial face. It doubled down its efforts, more leaves than he had hands, fighting him back. He bled from various locations, blood dripping down into his hair.

Tristan had gashes on his face and across his chest, his shirt badly ripped and both colors of his blood oozing down his skin. He yanked at its head petals, but instead of coming off, they jerked the flower head around as if they were hair. He scratched at the area where an eye should've been, but it did no good.

"Call them off, Jessie," Sebastian said urgently. "Hurry. We're running out of time."

I shifted back into my human form. "Back off, guys," I said, trying to instill my voice with urgency and command without shouting. "Back off!"

Tristan stepped away, panting hard. He flexed and unflexed his fingers.

"I need healing, Jessie," he said with a growl. "It got a bite in. Its poison is potent."

I got to work immediately, but Dave darted forward for another go at the flower, clearly in the grips of what had become a personal vendetta.

"Dave, back off," I said, zapping him with magic. "Stop!"

Austin lunged forward to help, and Tristan took the cue to lend his aid, but I signaled for them both to stop as I stepped between the basajaun and the flower.

"Jess, no!" Austin knocked over the rope stand to get to me, running into my wall of magic instead.

Dave tried to reach around me and grab the flower's neck, but I blocked him and then pushed at his chest.

"Stop, Dave!" I shoved a little more, helped by stinging magic. "Stop!"

He blinked in confusion and frustration, his hands still up, but I had his attention.

"We're going to try something else," I told him. "Edgar likely has more of these things back at Ivy House. You have my permission to try and kill one of those if you like, but right now we need to sort this out in a hurry, and Sebastian has an idea."

Dave's eyebrows drooped, and he huffed out a breath through his nostrils, not at all happy about the turn of events, but he stepped back.

Austin was there, putting his hand on Dave's shoulder and quickly moving him away from me.

"It's fine." I pushed Austin a little to make room. "He's fine, relax. We don't need any more testosterone shoved up in this mess. It'll just set him off again."

"Okay, Jessie, quickly—" Sebastian glanced across at the other flower, now issuing a low, constant hiss in our direction. "Right, so instead of trying to eradicate these things immediately, which doesn't seem to be working anyway, we can just cage them in."

"What do you mean?"

He worked his hands and started muttering, and I quickly caught on to the spell he was using. He'd tweaked it, but I knew the basics. When he looked to me for help, I joined him in the casting. Sweat was beading my brow by the time he finally nodded, and we released the spell together.

A hazy pinkish shine wavered in front of the more

aggressive flower. It immediately struck out, hitting the spell as though it was a solid wall.

"No, start again," Sebastian said. "Let's make it bigger."

We did it again, working quicker now. It completely encircled the flower this time. We backed off and the surly flower settled down slightly, watching us, not hitting the confines of its new magical prison.

Austin righted the rope around the exhibit, something the other exhibits didn't have—Edgar's half-hearted attempt at protecting visitors. Austin made the enclosure a bit larger than before, giving the flowers more space.

The flower watched him until he stepped away, Tristan with him. In a moment, it started to sway calmly. They apparently didn't hold grudges.

I puffed out a breath. "Good thinking," I told Sebastian, shifting my gaze to the other Attack Flower 3.0. "How close do we have to get to use the spell? I've thrown it through the air before, but this casting was more complex."

Talking echoed around us. I glanced at the clock. The judges had to be just around the corner. The fair itself would open in another fifteen minutes. We had to solve this now. *Right now.*

"Let's see if we can just..."

"Here." Nathanial quickly stripped and shifted, reaching out to Sebastian.

"This won't be noticeable at all," Sebastian

murmured sarcastically, turning around and lifting his arms.

"No, no." I gestured Ulric forward. "Smaller is better. Nathaniel's wings would reverberate throughout the whole space." Ulric quickly stripped down. "If he and I stay by the wall, we'll be magically hidden. That should be close enough to cast that spell, right?"

"*You'll* be hidden. I'll be floating in midair while applying a magical jail cell around an attack flower," Sebastian said.

"Wait, here." Nessa handed Sebastian a little vial. "Get invisible. *Quickly*. Someone is literally right around the corner."

Sebastian drank it down as Ulric lifted him into the sky. I transformed and followed them a moment later, cursing my shimmery pink-purple wake as I crossed over the flower exhibit. It was a testament to how supportive we all were of each other that we weren't just tramping through the flowers and dealing with this on foot. Then again, I would've been naked. That likely would have been noticed if I'd stayed in human form.

We got to work near the wall, the tingling of magic telling me my gargoyle powers had kicked in, and I was blending into the stone and concrete behind me. Sebastian worked quickly, pushing me, much more experienced and just all around better. I kept up, barely, adding the needed power.

"Edgar, go stall them," Nessa said through her teeth, shoving him toward a gush of laughter. "Hurry!"

He disappeared in a flash of movement, and seconds later his voice carried to us. We worked frantically and released the spell just as Edgar skulked around the corner with five people. The three men wore ill-fitting suits, while one of the women had on what was either a flowy pant suit or a flowered skirt down to her ankles. Middle-aged and older, all of them had clipboards and smiles, chatting and having a good time.

Those smiles dripped off their faces as they saw what Edgar had in store for them.

The spell finished locking around the flower. The flower poked forward, hitting its cage and simultaneously drawing the attention of the people walking toward the exhibit.

"Did that..." A man with thinning gray hair styled in a combover pointed at the flower. His brow furrowed.

"What was that, Dick?" another of the guys asked, a very fitting name.

Ulric flew upward a bit and then headed sideways, careful not to make sound. I followed, sticking to the wall.

"Oh. Look." The woman in the flowered skirt pointed at Jasper, standing in front of the others. "A few of the cheering squad put on capes."

"That is because of the gargoyle theme," Edgar said, rubbing his hands together. "In myth, it's said that when a gargoyle is in its human form, their wings turn into large capes down their backs. I thought it might be fun to cosplay a bit."

"Then why aren't you wearing a cape?" the other woman asked, a crease forming between her eyebrows as she caught sight of the main statue.

"Oh no, don't be silly." Edgar laughed. "I would never presume to impersonate so great a being as a gargoyle."

"He's laying it on a little thick," Niamh muttered. "I regret this whole joke."

"I should hope so," Mr. Tom replied indignantly. "Those flowers are a menace."

"Are ye daft? Those weren't my doing! Fierce useful, though, if ye were to plant them all around Kingsley's place. That'd give the coming"—she hesitated, sliding a glance at the coming judges—"*outsiders* a shock."

Ulric and I landed softly, Sebastian stepping forward to get out of the way while the two of us quickly shifted. Nessa wandered back over, pretending to randomly survey the wall, and gave Ulric his clothing. She handed me two vials.

"Your clothes couldn't be salvaged," she whispered and handed me a vial. "This is to strip away the revealing potion." I took it, and she held out another. "This is to apply the invisibility potion to yourself."

You couldn't have both potions at the same time or they nulled each other, something Sebastian was working on fixing.

I took the first and then waited a bit as everyone

moved out of the way and allowed Edgar to lead the judges to the focal point of his exhibit.

"Ah yes, I see, gargoyles," one of the men said, looking everything over. "Interesting. Haunting, even. The statue in the middle is even...*off*. Do you see that? It's like...things aren't quite in the right places."

"Oh yeah." The woman with the flowered shirt cocked her head. "Odd."

"Yes. That is the gargoyle god, carved by hand," Edgar said.

He continued to explain his design elements as I took the other potion. Austin made his way to me, clearly having no interest in the design elements that made up Edgar's masterpiece. Tristan was right behind him, drawing the attention of all the judges.

"Yes, didn't he do a great job dressing up?" Edgar asked, putting out a hand to stop Tristan. "It's like he just stepped off the battlefield."

Tristan looked at the hand, and his whole bearing vibrated with warning. His wings fluttered ever so slightly, and his pecs, bloodied from his encounter and peeking through a large rip in his shirt, flexed.

"The king of the gargoyles, right here," Edgar said wistfully, dropping his hand. "If only I could've stuck him in the exhibit, right?"

"How did you get your eyes to glow?" one of the people asked, but Tristan didn't stick around for a question and answer session. He glanced at me as he stopped next to Austin. Through our gargoyle bond I could feel his anger and concern as his gaze did a quick sweep of my body. Seeing nothing, he glanced away, tracking some people down the way as they stopped and surveyed what was probably their exhibit. They began fluffing up some moss.

"Look!" Combover exclaimed. "Look, the plant is moving! At first I thought my eyes were playing tricks, but no, if you watch closely, they move!"

"He needs to tweak them so they appear to be moving with a breeze, not on their own," Tristan said softly, presumably not wanting the judges to overhear. "If they are moving independently of the environment around them, the enemy will notice them."

"Agreed," Austin responded. "They also need to look more like actual sunflowers. Helluva concoction, though."

"Helluva concoction," Tristan agreed.

The rest of the team wandered toward us, and it turned out Edgar *did* plan to hang around indefinitely to watch his flowers. I wasn't sure if that was to protect fair goers, or because he just wanted to see people's reactions to his display. Either way, I told him he could stay so long as he didn't get arrested or caught using magic, and he promised to call if something went wrong with the magic containing those flowers.

One thing was for sure, Edgar would not be participating in any more week-long flower competitions in non-magical areas, so he'd better soak it up.

SEVEN

Nessa

An hour and a half or so after the hot mess of the flower show, Nessa jogged out the front door of Ivy House, toward the car, wanting to grab her notepad. On the steps, she stutter-stopped as she caught sight of a large shape sitting by himself, looking out at the empty street.

A too-small T-shirt stretched across Tristan's mighty shoulders, the seams straining in their fight to stay together. Holes had been cut out for his wings, and the arm holes pulled tight around his biceps. Austin was a large dude, but he didn't have the height or breadth of this massive gargoyle-monster.

"Hey," she said, slowing down to stand beside him. "How's it going? I love your baby doll T."

He didn't glance up, and after a moment, it became clear he didn't plan on responding.

Confused because he rarely missed a chance to tease or be teased by her, she sat down beside him. Elbows on her knees, she looked out at the street with him. Nothing remotely interesting to look at other than a car backing out of a driveway. Niamh was the only one who habitually sat out on her porch in this neighborhood, and she'd removed herself to Austin's pub after they'd gotten back from the fair. She was largely being blamed for the whole fiasco, including the embarrassing display of that statue and the various little gargoyles perched in the exhibit.

Nessa started chuckling. She couldn't help it. That flower show had been so aggressively out of the range of normal behavior that if they'd invited mages to witness it, the mages would've all thought they'd be murdered in some gruesome way in that pavilion. That's how much it would have unsettled them.

Actually, that was an amazing idea. After the fair, that statue needed to ride again!

"Just taking in the day, huh?" Nessa asked, calming down a little to match his apparently somber mood.

"Taking a break."

"Ah." She nodded and let silence linger for a moment. "Mr. Tom made some sandwiches. Did you get one?"

"No."

She nodded again, allowing the silence to stretch

this time, wondering if he needed to talk. Or maybe needed someone else to talk. He was hard to read.

"I had one," she said, monitoring him out of the corner of her eye to see if he tensed in annoyance. "They were a little dry because Mr. Tom ran out of mayonnaise. He had to use butter instead. He'd said as much when I first entered the kitchen, but Ulric and Jasper came in late. So on the sly, I asked Ulric—very seriously, of course—if Niamh had dropped off the sandwiches because they didn't seem like Mr. Tom's. He, of course, asked Jasper about it, who blurted it out because that's what he does." She started laughing again. "You should have seen how indignant Mr. Tom got!"

He turned his head to look at her.

His eyes glowed in that way they did, like embers in a dark night. His gaze roamed her face slowly, taking her in. It didn't seem sexual, though. His notice didn't stop on her lips or dip down to her body. Instead, he focused on her eyes, his look deep and soul-searching.

She leaned forward and rested her cheek on her arms, looking back at him. "Do you want a sandwich? I can go get you one. He made...a ridiculous amount of them. I have no idea why. I think he's a little shaken up about Edgar."

"Why?" Tristan whispered.

"Well..." She straightened up again, trying to remember Ulric's gossip. He'd somehow gotten it from Patty, which was insane because they'd only been home a half hour and Patty hadn't even gone to the fair.

Nessa had no idea how she'd pieced it all together so quickly. The woman was a marvel.

"I guess before all of this," she said, "Mr. Tom kinda looked after Edgar and made sure he didn't get into any trouble. Before Jessie, I mean. Then Jessie came, and Mr. Tom's priorities shifted. He still mostly kept track of Edgar, to make sure he didn't stray too incredibly far from...reality, we'll say, but lately there has been so much going on that he kinda lost sight of him. First there was the gnome invasion and now the killer flowers. I guess Mr. Tom feels slightly responsible. It seems that Edgar isn't one to let out of your sights for long. He's surprised many an enemy, actually. He's bonkers but incredibly wily in a pinch."

Tristan continued to look at her, and she found that she didn't mind the notice. There was no expectation in it, no pressure. No request for her to perform or dependency on her sunshine. Just a look, taking her in.

"I thought the hardest part of this position would be working with the shifters," he said after a while, looking down the street again. "They're similar, but just different enough to make things tedious. That's the way it seemed, anyway. Turns out that part's simple. Alpha Steele is a strong and sure leader, with a firm handle on his people and his duty. He's open minded enough to take our differences in stride. Working with him has been a pleasure."

She followed his lead, looking out over the street again.

"I'd gotten the impression that he handled most of

the territory," he went on, "and Jessie handled her very small crew. It seemed to me—and all the gargoyles during our visit—that his job was much more robust. He was essentially the leader, and she was the mate with magic. He took care of her, coddled her, and she did spells or whatever it was the house had granted her."

"And now?" she prompted, not having heard all of that before.

He huffed, kicking his feet down the last step to the ground and leaning back.

"I didn't know what the hell I was doing back there," he spat out. "I've led guardians into battle. I've traveled the wilds. I've dealt with much worse than attacking flowers. But if I had been in charge of that clusterfuck, it would've all gone to hell. Flowers would've killed people, Dicks and Janes would've witnessed it, the exhibit would have exploded, and the basajaun would likely be rampaging through the fairgrounds or something, I don't know." Surprising her, he started to laugh. "I felt like I was standing around with my dick in my hand, wondering what to do next and wishing I'd let Alpha Steele handle it from the beginning."

"What does that have to do with your perception of Jessie?"

"Alpha Steele cannot lead her crew, as small as they are. I can't. We'd both try, and we'd both fail. He as much as admitted that to me on the way back here. Jessie manages all of these powerful people, full of aggression and idiosyncrasies, without seeming to. She gives them enough space to go berserk—but not so much that she can't call them down if she needs to. She's balancing her crew on this incredibly dangerous precipice that she doesn't seem to realize is abnormal. This, in her mind, is a normal day. She thinks all this craziness around her is just that, craziness. Weirdness."

"And you don't." She didn't make it a question.

He leaned forward again, looking over at her. "Do you?"

"I think it is delightfully weird, yes. Mages tend to fear that which they don't understand. Her crew is basically our dream scenario. Her crew's weirdness will actually keep her safe when we go into the snake pit. I think it's a blessing. The fact that she *can* call them down is enough for me. She stepped in front of an enraged basajaun today without batting an eye. She trusted him not to hurt her. And you know what? He didn't. You need to have faith, Tristan. That's a hard thing to grasp, I know, especially since you spent so long under the leadership of someone you couldn't trust, but it's safer than trying to control things."

"Have faith in her crew?" he asked quietly. "The same crew that called in mages to attack her?"

Those words stung. "I'm not in her crew, remember?"

His brow arched. "So I shouldn't trust you?"

She tried for any easy smile, but it wouldn't come. Then, to her surprise, she found herself answering. "No. No one should trust me."

"And why is that?"

"Because when I am traveling through hell, and that is almost always because of the life I lead, I have a habit of pulling on the devil's whiskers."

He studied her for a long time, then tsked. "Natasha, Natasha." His smile was pure evil. "You have no idea what hell is."

Her return smile was condescending, but she stopped herself before she could say something else she might regret, like more truths. He had too much information about her already, not to mention a few secrets she wished he didn't know.

Instead, she grabbed his arm to haul him up. "Come on."

He resisted, barely flexing to do so. A soft rip issued from his shirt as she stumbled. Her foot slipped off the step, throwing her off balance. She staggered against his leg, tripped over his foot, and tumbled down on top of him.

He caught her easily, spinning her in his arms like she was as light and malleable as a pillow, then cradling her against his chest.

"I give the orders, little one," he said in that whisky voice, smooth and wicked. His amber eyes flashed, and when his gaze roamed her face this time, it did settle on her lips. His breath smelled like chocolate and his body carried the scent of mountain rain and fabric softener.

Her core tightened but adrenaline spiked, his size and strength whispering of dangerous secrets and hidden depths. Her fingers itched for her knife, but her body ached to be dominated into sweet oblivion.

He wasn't the kind of guy to be taken for a ride and then cast away, though. He wasn't the kind of guy who'd tolerate flirty plays and head games. He'd see right through those. No, he was the kind of guy who ate souls and sinfully consumed his prey. Decadently. Erotically. Absolutely.

He was the kind of guy she could not, under any circumstances, get involved with. Not for a weekend. Not even for a night. When a guy had the confidence to swing around his big dick energy like some sort of weapon, a girl needed to steer clear or face the consequences. She was no fool. Because his look right now said any entanglement with him wouldn't be about hearts and flowers. It would be pure, carnal sin, and she would never get enough.

"Done?" she asked flippantly, knowing better than to struggle to get away. He'd release her when he was ready. He'd make a show of it. God that was so hot, just her speed. Too bad he was who he was. Or what he was, maybe.

A sinful smile curled his lips. "If you like." He stood with her, holding her for a moment longer and then depositing her onto the ground. "Where did you want to take me?"

"Oh, now you want to come?"

His eyes darkened. "I always want to come, Natasha. I'll make sure you do, too."

She'd walked into that one.

She ticked her head back toward the house. "Come with—" She shook her head. Usually she was the dirty one. She wasn't used to the role reversal. "Follow me."

Inside the door, she stopped.

"Are you sure you don't want a sandwich? I could just go and grab one, and we'll be on our way."

"Sure, since you're offering."

That voice was so smooth and rich, so utterly annoying in her current headspace. She needed to release a little pent-up steam. It had been a while. Maybe she'd hit the bar after this and find one of the gargoyles who wouldn't want her number after the deed was done.

In the kitchen, Jessie and Austin were discussing the attack flowers. Jessie looked up when Nessa ran in.

"How's Tristan?" she asked, her worry evident. "Did we scare him away? He's been a little off."

"You guys threw him into the deep end. He's just... trying to adjust. I'm going to show him the updates to the art room. He likes those paintings."

"We're about to check out the attack flowers in the wood," Austin said. "If he wants to skip it, I can meet him back here for a game of pool."

"Oh..." Nessa stalled in grabbing a sandwich from the towering stack Mr. Tom had set out. "Has the pool room been refurbished?"

"No," he replied. "It's still serviceable, though. The table is level and the cues are good quality and straight."

"Ah, Nessa, back for more?" Mr. Tom said, entering the room. "Fantastic. I have—"

"Nope," Jessie said.

Mr. Tom froze halfway through pulling down an espresso cup. He then lifted it back up. "I have lots of sandwiches, or I can make you something else?"

"Just grabbing a bite for Tristan. He missed lunch." She reached for a plate for the sandwich she held.

"Oh, how could you?" Mr. Tom was there in a moment, slapping her hand that held the sandwich.

"What—" Nessa tried to shy away only to have Mr. Tom wrestle the sandwich from her.

"Just give in," Jessie said. "It's easier on everyone that way."

"I..." Nessa let go and then took a step back as Mr. Tom shooed her away.

"I will make him a plate and deliver it shortly. Go."

Back with Tristan, she lifted her hands in apology. "Sorry, Mr. Tom will be delivering your food. I wasn't quick enough to escape him. The alpha invited you to pool after they check out the attack flowers. You're suddenly a popular guy."

He smiled and minutely shook his head, stepping aside as she led the way to the stairs. She could tell his mood had shifted again, back to reserved and quiet. Contemplative.

"I get why you're overwhelmed," she said as they reached the top of the second floor and she directed them toward the next set of stairs. "It's one thing to deal with an attack flower. It's another to gear up for a small outing with a bunch of Dicks and Janes and suddenly find yourself tasked with killing a magical flower, of all things, while a basajaun rages beside you—it was a lot."

"It shouldn't have been."

"Oh no? That sounds like a normal day where you come from?"

He was quiet as they reached the top of the stairs and made their way to the new art hall, which was actually just a large room. Naomi had deemed "art room" an unworthy title, though.

"It wasn't just what happened today," he finally said. "Maybe it's the generosity of this place that's throwing me off. I can show up at any time, at any hour, and Mr. Tom will be there to offer me food, or a drink, or an expensive car to drive like it's no big deal."

She tried the handle and found it wouldn't budge.

"Really, Ivy House? I'm not going to steal anything and he knows better." Nessa tried the handle again, and this time it turned. "I'm appalled that you would even question."

"I feel like I'm being setup or something," he said. "Like this is some sort of trap. It's too good to be true."

She laughed. "Guilty conscience. Jessie and Austin are as above board as you're going to get. They don't play games. Most of Austin's shifters don't either. Some of Jessie's crew? Yeah, maybe. Depends on if you mind your manners. Where's that shirt of mine you took, by the way?"

Nessa, Sebastian and the basajaun Phil had taught some shifters a lesson for picking on Ulric. Tristan had smelled the blood on her and taken the shirt, incriminating evidence. The guy was morally gray at best—she worried how he'd use the blackmail.

"Next to my bed with the blood stains cut out and your smell still lingering. Want to know where the body is buried?"

She paused as the door swung open, looking back at him with surprise. "You didn't."

She hadn't asked about Ulric's attackers since then, but she hadn't seen any of them in the bar since. She'd hoped they'd had a decent enough scare and knew to stay away. But maybe...

Tristan pushed past her and into the room. "Dead men tell no tale—"

The breath left him as he surveyed the room. A statue stood in the middle with benches positioned around it, the actual statue nothing of consequence but the position of it lending the room a little *je ne sais quoi* —or so Naomi said. The room had been painted just slightly off-white with crown molding lining the ceiling and floor. The floor had been sanded, stained, and polished, and the whole place smelled new.

Each painting had been looked up, cataloged, valued, and put in a better or different frame. After that, it was hung in whichever way Naomi thought best. Little chairs and benches had been arranged around the room so visitors could sit and view the pieces.

At waist level around the room, old books were displayed in temperature controlled glass cases. All of them had some significance other than their age. In the front corner stood a coat of arms, which was old and rustic and super cool, and a sword was positioned in the back. Whence they came, Nessa couldn't say, but Naomi was pleased about their authenticity.

Tristan started forward immediately, ignoring the statue after a cursory glance and heading instead to the first painting on his right.

"Hello?" she asked, not able to help her fascination at the emotions flickering across his face. "Tell me you didn't kill him."

"I didn't kill him."

"Don't lie."

He shrugged, offering no comment this time.

"Why?" she asked, shoving his arm.

His voice was subdued, reverent. "These pieces are incredible. I didn't get to see many of them before."

"You were too busy staring at the gold in the closet downstairs. *Why?* That could put Ulric in danger."

"Ah. So you were doing it for Ulric? Hmm." He moved on to the next. "I initially sought him out to see if he had endangered you in any way, or if he would talk about your altercation with him. I killed him because he insulted you."

"Okay. Well, that was on you."

"I didn't get rid of the bloodstains from that shirt. I did cut them out...but I put them somewhere for safe-keeping. Shifters have a very keen sense of smell. Your delicious fragrance mixed with his blood won't look good for you."

She ground her teeth. "Look at me," she demanded.

He dutifully turned and did so. In a moment, he bent with an infuriating smile.

"You'll do the most damage if you hit me in the jugular," he offered. "Or maybe go for your knife. I'll let you attempt to get it into my heart."

The fact that he could tell she wanted to punch him enraged her further. "I'm going to bring Cyra to your house, or wherever you live—"

"Don't pretend you don't know where I live."

She froze.

His smile was knowing. His voice dropped an octave. "Don't pretend you haven't peered into my windows. Why do you think I leave the blinds in my bedroom open now? Peer inside any time you like."

One time she'd peered in! It had just been *one time,* after she'd followed him back to his house and snuck around the premises. She'd wondered if he'd be able to feel her essence from so far away. And then she'd drifted toward the light like a moth to a flame, finding him getting ready for bed, naked, glistening—

"Oh shut up." She stormed from the room.

She needed a better game plan where he was concerned. He was playing her like a fiddle. It was exasperating.

EIGHT

Austin

"Tristan." Austin walked into the billiard room, finding the other man with his T-shirt literally ripping at the seams. "Jess'll have Mr. Tom order you some shirts in your size, be it button-down or T-shirts. Whatever you need."

The large gargoyle turned from the far corner of the room, revealing a painting in a wooden frame behind him.

"Did my grandma Mimi leave some art out of the art room?" Austin asked, crossing to the rack of cue sticks mounted on the wall.

"Yes, I think she did. I can't be certain, but that one might be a lost piece of history."

"Do you like art?"

"Very much." He met Austin at the rack.

"Have you spoken to Mimi? It's one of her passions. I'm sure she'd love to talk to a fellow connoisseur."

Tristan waited for Austin to select his pool stick and get out of the way before studying the selections.

"Sir, may I ask a question?" he asked.

"We're off duty, Tristan. Your gargoyle culture is a lot more relaxed than my shifter culture. Ivy House is more relaxed still. I've gotten used to letting down my guard here. When we're here, in private company, feel free to address me as Austin."

Tristan ran his fingers along one of the cue sticks. "We shouldn't be using these. I will, because I can't help myself, but they're relics out of time. Do you have any idea what a collector would pay for these? In this condition?"

"A passion for billiards as well, huh? Should I prepare to be spanked?"

"Probably." Tristan grinned over his shoulder. "Care to put money on it?"

"Sure. Assuming you finally choose a stick."

He shook his head but selected one.

Instead of asking whatever had been on his mind, Austin reached for the chalk in silence. Something was clearly troubling the gargoyle, but he figured it would be best to work around to it. Tristan didn't seem the type to open up easily. Maybe not at all, given his past and Niamh's inability to find out anything about it. She'd gotten another clue earlier, though, with the nightmare-inducing magic. She'd figure out everything, given enough time.

"How do you feel about the flower incident at the fair?" Austin asked, a good entry point into a conversation.

Tristan surveyed the table, rested his stick flat upon it, and then rolled it. Satisfied that it was straight, he left it there and carefully pulled the balls out of the pockets and collected them at the end.

"Conflicted. I failed. I saw you allowing it to happen, only stepping in when the mi—Jessie was in danger."

"I have limits."

"Of course. I apologize, I didn't anticipate her stepping in front of the—Dave."

"Neither did I. I've always had very shaky results when stepping in front of an enraged basajaun, and that's in my larger shifter form."

"I remember from the raid. Has she never seen them incensed?"

"Of course she has. She just..." Austin couldn't help but shrug. "She has a gut instinct about what people are capable of. And when it comes to her crew, she's never wrong. With outsiders, like gargoyle leaders or mages, she always expects the best, tends to be sorely disappointed, and reacts...in exciting ways."

Tristan waited until Austin had set up the balls before walking to the top of the table to break. He leaned over, lining up the cue ball, and from that simple movement it was clear he'd spent a great many hours doing just this. Probably for the last fifteen years. He hit them hard, scattering the balls across half the table and landing two, one stripe and one solid.

"What's the rule?" Tristan asked. "Do I choose stripes or solids now, or do I need to make another to determine it? Everyone seems to play differently."

Austin pretended to think about it. "Next ball chooses, I think." He had also played a lot of pool. A *lot* of pool. Let Tristan find out the hard way.

"She has a lot of live wires on her team." Tristan's shot was perfect, landing the ball and lining up the next shot.

"That's basically all she has, yes."

He hit the next—again, nearly perfect—but didn't quite line up his next shot. He'd falter soon.

"And she's cool with all of this?" He walked around the table, surveying the many shots he had at his disposal. Stalling.

"All of what?"

"The various species." He shook his head, staring blankly at the pool table. "The chaos."

"I usually run point," Austin said. "I've known a few of the players for a long time—Jess before she had magic, and the crew as it was being built. I've been eased into...what it is. Today, with you leading, was an experiment. I wanted to see if you'd only choose guys from your past cairn, how you'd do at integrating the guardians with her crew, how you'd organize transportation—the works. The guys you chose, only one of them from your past cairn, seemed shell-shocked."

"I chose the best guardians in this territory, and yes,

they were. I regret to say that I was, too. Still am. I have zero training for how to handle magical attack flowers at a non-magical county fair while still keeping the non-attack flowers in tip-top shape. The whole situation... was a bit of a mind-fuck, sir—Austin."

He hit the next ball, a little off. It missed just barely. Austin's turn.

"And you think I've had training for that type of situation?" he asked as he lined up his ball, then moved his stick a bit off center. He didn't want to show his skill so early. They hadn't put any money on this game yet. They hadn't agreed on a figure. He'd show strong when there was a purse to win.

"I think you're a little...more open-minded than I am."

"Only when it comes to Jess. I suggest you try to be, too. I know what the gargoyle leaders thought of our setup. What most people think. And then they see her in battle, or managing her crew like she did today, and they see a whole different side of her. That side has earned her respect in the pack. She has only been personally challenged one time, and that is because she met the challenge in a spectacular way. The thing to do with her and her crew is to follow her lead until you can figure out how to enhance it."

Tristan blew out a breath. "You have a lot of trust in her with all these powerful beings."

"She has a lot of trust in me to handle the territory around her. The two of us work in tandem. We each handle part of a whole. Soon I have every belief she'll be leading more of the gargoyle faction as I command the shifters. She just needs to work up to it. This is all new to her."

He cocked his head. "I see what you're saying, though I have no experience working with someone else that closely. I've never trusted anyone that much."

"It shows. I didn't take a leadership role until I was ready for one..."

Austin missed his next ball on purpose and Tristan smirked.

"Not very subtle, alpha," he said, moving into position for his next shot. Austin couldn't tell if the comment was about what he'd said or missing the shot. Maybe both.

"I've gotten clearance from Jessie to speak to Nathanial," Tristan said, lining up his shot. "That gargoyle's a fount of wisdom. He's quiet. He's smart. He watches everything and only steps in when he's needed. Where it gets interesting is that he always knows exactly when he's needed. I saw it today. I was hovering around like an idiot, and he stepped forward when it was crucial."

"Not totally true." Austin watched Tristan bank a shot. He missed the pocket he was going for but sunk his ball into a different pocket. Austin's turn, but the ball was still made. He sensed both of them were playing coy at showing their skills. "You pushed forward, asking to be needed—he waits until he's needed. You took the role I usually take. In fairness to him, I've never allowed him the opportunity to take that role."

"Why did you allow me?"

"Morbid curiosity?" They both laughed. "You have a host of guardians to command, more coming all the time. You need to understand Jess to do your job well. You also need to understand that her crew has the capacity to turn any situation strange. Nathanial knows when to step in, yes, and he's a fantastic flying helper for her. It's his biggest asset. But he's not a commander like you are."

Tristan didn't comment and instead they passed in silence for a time, hitting or missing their shots in a dance of pretend. They were both better than this, both circling each other. It felt like a metaphor for their current situation.

"Shall I cut to the chase?" Austin finally ventured, winning by sinking the black and letting Tristan rack the next game.

"Sure."

His tone was unmistakably wary.

"Actually, why don't you tell me your reservations. You think you made a mistake in coming here, is that it? Your last position—" He stopped when Tristan's body language changed, radiating unease and confusion.

He'd guessed wrong.

"Too many alphas, then," he guessed again. "You need to work with one or the other of us."

Austin broke, sinking one.

"Begging your pardon, alpha, may I be candid?"

"Of course."

"I'm having a hard time trusting all of this. The only one I do trust is Natasha, and she's probably the least trustworthy of you all. I *get* her, though. You all, with your fancy food and drink and easy lifestyle amid so much power and chaos—I don't understand any of this. Honestly, it feels like a trap. Like this can't possibly be real life. There are beings in this house right now who could kill me in half a second, and we're playing pool and waiting on drinks from a gargoyle who must have been a guardian at one time but is now an overbearing butler. My mind is spinning."

Austin stared at him for a moment, just to make sure he was genuine, and then started laughing. He knew this man wouldn't challenge him because of it or think he lacked the control to hold it back.

"I will never speak ill of Nessa," he finally said, collecting himself. "It's not easy to be a low-magic mage playing with the big dogs. She's a survivor, and a survivor in her situation has to make some grisly decisions. I don't fault her for that. She's got a good heart with a lot of pain and guilt in her past. I don't know specifics and I won't ever ask. Her partner in crime, Sebastian, is the same way. Even though he loves Jess like a sister, he's as dangerous to us as he is necessary to Jess. When it comes to them, don't think I am blind. They are very good at what they do but very bad at hiding their thoughts from people who excel at reading body language. I can trust them because I can read them. If there is someone not to trust, it is Patty,

Ulric's mother. Lovely woman, but one conversation will have you giving her safe combinations. Everyone else—honestly, they aren't hard to get a handle on if you're paying attention. You know when Cyra is going to burn you alive, for example. She's not subtle. Hollace cannot be provoked. I've had many shifters try. Ulric never gives in. Nessa cares more than she'd like to admit, which she showed by dealing with Ulric's bullies. Jasper can keep a secret. Niamh is incredible at manipulation and loyal to an absolute fault. If you're not in her circle, you'd best watch yourself because she can be dangerous when she wants to be. Mr. Tom picks up the slack with everyone in the crew. Edgar is... Well. You've seen enough of him yourself to know. He's ingenious and incredibly...not right in the head. None of them are hard to read, Tristan. So what is it you can't trust? Your own ability to see details?"

Tristan stared at him like he had two heads. "You're not blind," he repeated, and Austin heard the question behind it.

"No," he replied. "I didn't know specifics, but I knew mages were about to attack our territory. It came as a welcome surprise when you all suddenly decided to stay. I had a feeling it wasn't a coincidence, especially since you changed your people's configuration and placement both inside and outside of the territory. It was pretty clear you were setting up a warning system and planned to help us. I worked within that understanding."

Tristan had a look of shock on his face. He lowered the pool stick, still staring.

"You were the instigator in staying, right?" Austin asked. "I figured you must have been since your leader had no interest in Jess or our territory. Why did you decide to keep people here?"

He shook his head. "Partially a favor. Partially to see a female gargoyle and your territory in battle. I wanted to see if I would stay and be a part of it. Why didn't you tell Jessie? That doesn't sound like an open, trusting relationship."

"She probably would've insisted on telling the gargoyle leaders. I knew from Nathaniel that the guardians would want to stay and do battle, but the leaders would have probably sited a grievance and taken off on principle. I couldn't let that happen. I wanted to showcase our battle strength as well as get some much-needed help. You staying made that possible."

Tristan's expression hardened. "So this whole territory," he said, "is essentially keeping Jessie in the dark about everything?"

Austin couldn't help chuckling as he took his turn. He sunk one easily, lining up for the next.

"Not even remotely. This is the only thing I've kept from her. I didn't tell her after the fact because she would have given it away to the mages, and I can't allow that to happen. Nessa and Sebastian basically gave me a roadmap of how they operate when the gargoyles came to town. Both of them are great at speaking lies, but neither of them have the body language to back that up. They seem to have one foot in our camp, one foot out. It's that foot out I need to watch. I will do anything to protect my mate and my territory. I need them to think they fooled me so they won't try any harder to fool me next time."

Tristan shook his head slowly, and damned if respect hadn't kindled in his eyes.

"Who knows about this?" he asked.

"Brochan, Kace, Niamh. Now you. Niamh was the one who figured out something was up. Together, we surmised what it was."

"Why are you telling me?"

"Because it's important for you to know all of this so you can do your job correctly and keep my mate, the most important thing in my life, safe. You need to get good at reading incredibly subtle body language. Shifters will show you how. A whole different world opens up when you can read the subtle cues."

"And if I tell the mages?"

"I don't think you're that stupid."

He paused for a moment. "No," he said softly, his eyes glowing brightly. "She thinks they sold you hook, line, and sinker."

"I know."

"She has a lot of respect and love for your mate, though. You should know that. Natasha was fighting her guilt over the situation when she asked me to stay longer. She'd already told me to put my trust in Jessie. I think they were genuinely trying to help."

"And that is why they are not dead."

Tristan nodded slowly, his eyes glimmering now. "This is the first I've seen of this side of you. I was starting to think you were too much of a boy scout. Natasha seems to think so."

Austin sank the next ball and then one after that, forgetting to pretend to be bad.

"I have a very dark past, actually. I was a nightmare in my youth. So much so that I almost killed my own brother." He tapped the pocket where he'd drop the black ball, and then did it with a hard shot. He straightened up, as serious as the grave. "When I said I'd do anything to protect my mate and my territory, I meant it. Jess is the rainbows and flowers half of our pairing, but even she has a deep darkness within her, too, created and churned by her gargoyle. In life, we are open and honest people, trying to do right by our pack. In war, we will not hold back. I see the same sort of darkness in you. You'll fit here, no problem. I ask that you fit *on* our team, and not against it."

Tristan started gathering the balls. "One thing, though."

Austin waited.

"Why am I given so many perks? Free food, fast cars, the white glove treatment whenever I'm here..."

"Because that is how they do things here. Have you ever gotten a free drink at my bar? A free meal at any of my restaurants?" Tristan leaned against the pool table, watching Austin silently. "Jess is treating you like family, and she is the matriarch of this family. She takes care of her own. She sees it as her duty, but it's actually just her way. And because she's so open and accepting, so are her people. Everyone in the crew gets those perks, and with them you have to deal with the oddity of this place and these people. Trust me, it's an even trade."

Tristan huffed out a laugh, going back to the balls.

"That was your big concern?" Austin asked, rubbing the chalk across his cue stick. "Too many perks?"

He shrugged. "It's unusual. I wondered if you were...setting me up, I don't know. Sounds stupid when I say it now, but..."

"Were you really treated that badly in the cairn?"

"We weren't treated badly. We just...weren't pampered. There's a difference."

"I suppose there is."

He stepped out of the way for Austin to break. "Does Jessie know you set up Ulric?"

"I didn't set up Ulric. I heard he was in some trouble and had my people watch out for it. When my people went to step in, Ulric asked them to leave it be. I think he thought word would get out that he needed help and other people would pick on him. I've heard he didn't always have it easy in his cairn growing up."

"A lot of the smaller guys don't. I stopped it in our cairn, as much as I could, but it was unusual for anyone to intervene."

"That's why it kept going on here, I think. Jasper

wouldn't say anything, and Ulric wanted to handle it himself. I left him to it."

"Then why did Natasha step in?"

Austin gave him a quirked eyebrow. "Haven't you been listening? Jess is the reason. She worried something was up, asked for Nessa's help, and Nessa handled it. My people found the blood and recognized all the scents. As I said, I'm not blind. I know what goes on in my territory. Strange thing, though. Everyone walked away from the altercation that night. Well...walked or limped. Yet, a few days later, the original perpetrator was nowhere to be found. He seems to have vanished."

"Strange. Maybe he realized he was picking on the wrong people and took off."

"Maybe," Austin said noncommittally, and they both knew he suspected Tristan had played a hand in that disappearance. He'd been incredibly discreet, leaving no scent trails to follow or any hint of foul play. Austin had absolutely no proof. He just had a hunch. This guy was good, and even now, his body posturing gave nothing away. This was why Niamh hadn't been able to get much on him. He was well practiced in shrugging off scrutiny.

"Anyway," Austin said, moving around the table. "That shifter was a disgrace. He dug his own grave. Someone just did him a favor and threw him into it. I was only surprised Ulric wasn't the person who did it."

"He should've. He's small, but he's a good guardian. He would've been more than capable."

"Agreed."

They played in amicable silence for a while, finally putting money down. Austin won the next game. When Tristan was racking, he finally spoke again, his tone friendly and light.

"So you need to put your woman's ex in his place, huh?"

Austin leaned his hands onto the pool table. "Technically, he hasn't done anything wrong. But speaking of reading body language—Jess's in this case—I think the guy has a lot of passive abuse to answer for over the years. He's a Dick, though, so I can't just beat the hell out of him."

"What's the plan?"

"Tie up the loose ends I should've dealt with before now. Jess has been incredibly patient, not asking for signed documents or even a key to my place—our place, as soon as I make it official. Nessa will be managing the social media angle. Jess is supposed to take me out on a perfect date soon—long story, and I half wonder if I shouldn't wine and dine her instead. She certainly deserves to be pampered more than I do. It would probably look better for her on social media, too. Not that I see her letting me turn the tables on the date even if I tried. Regardless, I guess we're basically engaging in passive aggressive warfare to take the wind out of his sails."

"Until you see him in person?"

"*If* I do."

"And if you do...are you going to lean into him a little?" Tristan's grin was sly, his eyes shining brightly.

Austin matched it, readying to break the balls. "You bet I am. First we have to get invited to see them."

"If you make him jealous enough, he'll invite you so he can size you up," Tristan said. "He'll hate that another man is making her happy. Dicks aren't so different from shifters. This guy had a claim. He won't want to give it up without a fight, especially if he's controlling. Make him jealous, and he'll extend the invite, guaranteed."

NINE

Jessie

Not long after sunset, I braced myself outside of Austin's bar, butterflies swarming my belly, worried I might not be able to pull this off. He'd taken me on the perfect date once. I would now return the favor.

Hopefully.

My problem was that I wasn't great at coming up with thoughtful and sentimental gifts. I'd always asked my kid what he wanted for Christmas and his birthday. I never guessed.

This time I had to get it together enough to prove I knew Austin well enough to give him an experience he'd fondly remember.

No pressure.

"What are you standing around gawking at, *creature?*"

My nemesis, Sasquatch, stood across from me, sucking on the end of a cigarette. He scowled, waiting for an answer.

"You look like some sort of lost mountain man. Do you not own any mirrors?"

"Says the woman with lipstick on her teeth." He smirked at me, flicked his cigarette, and peeled off into the bar.

I took a step back quickly, bringing my finger up to my teeth. Then I remembered I hadn't applied lipstick, and the pale gloss I wore wouldn't show up on my teeth in the dark.

"Butthead," I said, finally entering the bar.

Austin stood on the customer side of the bar wearing a gray button-up shirt with the sleeves rolled up around his muscular forearms. One arm was bent, holding a beer, and he was in a conversation with a couple of shifters. He glanced over as I came in, sensing my arrival. He quickly did a double take, his shoulders swinging my way as though he couldn't help himself. His gaze roamed my body, taking in the low neckline of my sparkly dress and the high reaching slit up my thigh. I'd dressed sexy. My outfit wasn't incredibly fancy because of where we'd end up, but the do-me heels and tight, revealing dress were intended to heat up his blood.

A path parted in front of me, shifters and gargoyles alike giving me plenty of space. I received nods and salutations, everyone being very conscious about where their eyes went. By now they all knew alpha shifters weren't rational when it came to their mates, and Austin was more alpha than most.

Just thinking about it filled me with heat. My hips swayed as I walked toward him, taking my time, soaking in his notice. Desire raged through the bonds and his eyes glimmered as he looked everywhere at once.

"Hey, baby," I said, running my hand up his arm and over his shoulder.

His free arm fell around me, his hand low on my hip. The touch was possessive, and he leaned toward me in a silent display of his claim.

"You look beautiful, Jess," he murmured, glancing his lips across mine. "You take my breath away."

I placed my hand on the back of his neck and pulled him a little closer, deepening our kiss. I knew he'd appreciate the public display of affection. He liked affirming his claim for all to see.

"Do you want to stay for a drink?" I asked after I ended the kiss, still standing close.

His shook his head, leaning back just a bit so that he could look down at my chest. "I'd rather go somewhere private. I'm a man—it's easy to give me a perfect date. Just get naked."

I laughed and curled my fingers around the neck of his beer. Holding his gaze, I pulled it toward me slowly, running my tongue across the edge before wrapping my lips around the opening. My sip was slow and his eyes were hungry as he watched my mouth, no doubt wishing it was wrapped around something of his.

"We'll have plenty of time for that," I told him in a sultry voice, keeping the bottle. "Let's get out of here. I have something to show you."

His fingers dug into my hips as he pulled me closer. Our bodies connected, and I could feel his hardness through his jeans. His lips trailed along the side of my neck, and his teeth scraped across my shoulder. I shivered and clutched his shirt, closing my eyes and moaning softly.

Somewhere private suddenly sounded good. Very good. Except I wanted to keep him on edge all night. I wanted to tease him until he exploded and took me in a fit of passion. I had plans for it that I knew he'd like.

"Come on." I handed back his beer.

He was slow to take it, keeping our bodies close, ignoring the guys he'd been talking to just a moment before. They were shifters, though. They wouldn't be affronted.

"If it pleases m'lady," he whispered, finally relenting and taking the beer. He drained it, slipping between the guys and placing it on the bar. "After you."

I pulled his arm up and over my shoulder as we walked out, relishing in his heat and the delicious smell of his cologne. I could tell his focus was entirely on me, on staying close, and he barely noticed anyone we passed. That changed when we left the bar, turned the corner, and stepped into the parking lot. Suddenly he slowed.

"Okay, so I know you're not totally a car guy like your brother," I said. "But you're a guy who likes to go fast, and this is one of the fastest cars out there. So I thought you might like to find a track or something and see how fast you can go. It also looks awesome. Please don't kill yourself."

"You bought this...for me?" he asked. "Jess..."

He stopped beside it, pulling his arm from around my shoulders and bending to look in the driver's side window.

"That's not all." I smiled at him nervously before opening the door. It swung upward at a diagonal, insanely cool.

I picked up the little box I'd deposited on the driver's seat before going into the bar. Turning, I opened it and revealed his next gift. The street light was too far away for good visibility, though.

"Hang on," I said, bending and angling so the light from the car could illuminate the watch. "I know you're *definitely* a watch guy. I had Sebastian help me with this one. It's a unique piece crafted by a master for a charity auction. It's one of a kind, a collector's piece in its own right, but it means something more in the mage world. Sebastian said they'll take one look at this watch and assume a female bought it for you. They'll quickly realize that female was *me*. This watch will tell them I have unwavering faith in your ability to protect me and value you more highly than any of them." I straightened, holding the watch for him. "It seems like a lot of symbolism for a single watch, I know, but Sebastian insists that's how it will be perceived. And it's all true, Austin. When I'm with you, I know I never have to fear for my safety. You've been watching my back since before I was magical. Each time I've grown in power, you've grown right along with me. You crush any sort of challenge I lob your way, and you do it gracefully. Gladly. You are the greatest alpha in the world, I truly believe that, and I'm honored and humbled that you'd pick me as your mate. I also know that you are the greatest man. We could have nothing, no magic, no money, no territory, and it would be enough just to have you in my life. Having you is enough to make me feel like the luckiest woman in the world."

He took the watch slowly, but his eyes were locked with mine. His other hand came up, and he lightly traced the pad of his thumb down the center of my throat, making me shiver.

"No car or watch," he said softly, "could be better than hearing those words from you. I love you, baby."

His kiss was reverent and unhurried, blanketing me with his body's warmth, and he ended it by pulling me in tightly. "You make me feel like the greatest alpha," he said, rocking me a little. "You make me feel like a man."

He finally pulled away, his gaze lingering on the watch and then taking in the car.

"Luckiest woman in the world?" He chuckled as he circled the car. "Talk about the luckiest man. This is too much, Jess. The watch, the car—did Mr. Tom approve of this?"

"How dare you," I said with a smile, standing back so he could continue checking out the car. "And yes, he did. I don't think he cares about how much things cost, though. I tried to buy a fifty dollar bracelet online that looked nice and he canceled the order. He said that style was beneath me."

"And you let him?"

"Only after Mimi and then Ulric agreed with him. Ulric called it downright ugly. I felt attacked." I laughed. "In my old life I would've killed for a personal shopper. Now I can't get away from them."

He was staring at me from over the roof of the car, his expression unreadable and his emotions turbulent.

"Mimi?" he asked in a flat tone.

I held up my hands. "I'm not taking liberties. I know she'd throat punch people for less. She asked that I call her that. Well...commanded, more like. She pretty much barked it at me, stared me down until I agreed, and then went back to her office."

"She doesn't let anyone call her Mimi. Except blood relatives—my mom, me, my brother, and my niece and nephew."

"Oh, uhh..." Suddenly unsure, I started to fidget. "I don't have to call her that if it's a special thing. I didn't realize."

He leaned on the roof now, his eyes so incredibly soft. "She's telling you you're family, Jess. *Her* family. She's claiming you. Ernessa is going to be furious, and I am going to mercilessly rub this in Kingsley's face."

My heart swelled, but I grimaced at him. "I hope

this isn't going to create a rift with them or anything. It's really not a big deal."

"God I love you," he whispered, opening the passenger door and stepping aside, his gaze following the door's journey as it swung upward. "This car is *sleek.*"

The excitement in his voice was unmistakable. I let a smile peek through my uncertainty about the whole family nickname situation.

"Kingsley lost his mind when he saw a picture of the Bentley." Austin rounded the hood and then reached his hand into the driver's side to feel the leather on the headrest. "He had no reservations in cursing me. This might not be a collector's edition, but I guarantee you, when the danger is over, he will fly out here just to take it for a drive." His smile was radiant. "The little brother is catching up to the great alpha."

He pulled out his phone and reached for me, turning us so he could take a selfie. He kissed my temple before bending over his phone, logging into social media so he could post it.

"Kingsley is going to call the second he sees this, you watch." He turned to me again, the camera closer this time, getting just him and me. He took one of us smiling, and then one of him kissing me on the cheek, the pic coming out a little off-center and my laughter not making me look like I had eight chins and strange face lines for once. Miracles.

"*Now* can we go somewhere private?" Austin asked

me, crowding me against the car, his hardness sending delicious shivers through my body.

"Not yet," I said, stealing a kiss and then pushing him away.

His eyes sparked with desire at the treatment, his gaze turning predatory.

"Get in." I motioned at the driver's side door. "We're late, let's go."

I laughed at the look he gave me before getting into the car and pushing the button for the door to lower. It wasn't nearly as comfortable as the Bentley, or even the Volvo I had for driving around town (it was as ritzy as I'd let Mr. Tom go), but there was something to be said for the way the engine revved and the excited joy radiating from Austin as he backed out of the parking lot.

People on the sidewalk stopped, a couple giving us a thumbs up and the other gawkers staring at the car with their mouths open or nudging their friends.

"I definitely need to take this to the track," Austin murmured, stepping on the gas when we had a little room but pulling his foot off again almost immediately because the car got up to speed in a blink. "It's a waste driving it around town. Where to?"

I gave him directions for the long way, smiling whenever he leaned on the gas to see what the car could do.

"This is too much, though, Jess," Austin said, taking a turn blindingly fast. I clutched the door handle, my stomach flinging out of my body. "That watch, too. I know of that watch maker, so I know how much his stuff goes for at auction. It's too expensive."

"Not for the Ivy House heir." I affected Mr. Tom's voice. "*You have a responsibility to the house to uphold the very great prestige with which it has blessed you.*" I went back to my normal tone. "And that was when I was trying to buy a moderately priced bracelet. What *I* think is moderately priced, anyway. I have a different playbook now. It'll take a minute to catch up. Think of it as armor. If mages will actually read all those layers of meaning into the watch, like Sebastian says they will, it's not just worth it, it's necessary. This car, too. Mages will eventually come to visit. We need to look the part. They'll be a lot harder to impress than those gargoyles."

"Feels wrong to accept gifts of this magnitude."

"Or does it feel oh-so-good?"

His smile gave him away.

"Turn left here," I said, pointing at the road.

He did as I said, now having to slow down because we were outside of town on somewhat dark roads. The potential for animals to jump out in front of the car was high.

"So you've got your social media all set up and active?" he asked as I pointed for him to take a left.

"Yeah. At first it was mostly crickets, but post one picture with you in it and suddenly my old high school friends are coming out of the woodwork." I laughed.

"Any notice from your ex?"

I rolled my eyes and looked out the window. "No.

I'm over that. I'm happy where I am and don't care what he's up to. I'm good." I turned back and ran my hand up his arm to his shoulder. "I have a dream life right now."

"Except for the constant threat of dying..."

"I ignore that bit when I think about my dream life. Slow down here." I peered out the window and then checked my phone. "Yeah, right here."

"Are you taking me somewhere to kill me?"

"To use you first, obviously, what do you take me for? Use you and *then* kill you."

"It would be a pleasant way to go." He reached over, sliding his hand up my thigh and under my dress. "Let's pull over somewhere secluded. I want to take you on the hood of this car."

His fingers ran over my panties, applying pressure right where I needed it.

"No," I said breathily as he rubbed. "Not until after."

"After what?" he whispered, the car barely crawling along the deserted road, his fingers slipping into the side of my panties and sliding through my wetness.

"After the next thing." I let my head fall back as my eyes fluttered closed. Summoning all my will, though, I pushed his arm away. "Not yet. Not until later. And then I promise the wait will be worth it."

He pulled his hand away slowly before leaning toward me, pulling me into a scorching kiss. I moaned, lost for a moment, not wanting to come up for air. I didn't relent, though, pointing ahead of us with a now shaking hand.

Knowing how he was affecting me, he chuckled darkly.

A mile down the road, we turned into a gravel area on the outskirts of a shabby sort of park. It didn't have any equipment for kids to play on and the baseball diamond on the other side was in terrible shape. What it did offer, though, was a large picnic area that could easily house the group of shifters I'd invited.

Several cars and trucks were already parked in the lot, and a large bonfire sent swirling embers into the sky. Portable, battery-powered lanterns hung on little hooks to either side of a large metal BBQ, three guys standing in front with tongs or spatulas. Other people stood around or sat in the wooden chairs, chatting and laughing, holding plastic cups or cans of beer.

Austin shut off the car and stared out at the merriment for a moment—hesitating as if in indecision. His emotions through the bonds were muted, something I wasn't used to. Was he doing that purposely to keep them from me, or did he not feel anything at all?

Kace, Austin's longest friend in this territory, had said I could invite any shifters I wanted and it wouldn't matter where they sat in the pack hierarchy. BBQs were well-established outlets for shifters—an opportunity for them to let their hair down. Fighting was strictly prohibited and challenges were forbidden. Austin had mentioned as much a time or two, and he'd seemed to relax at the feast we'd been treated to on basajaunak land. I'd thought he might be missing this. I'd thought maybe he'd enjoy just being a shifter for the night, no bar and no alpha obligations, without having to make allowances for other species or my odd crew. Just doing what he knew.

Suddenly I wondered if I'd made a huge mistake.

TEN

Austin's screen lit up, resting in the center console. He picked it up, unlocked it with his face, and then grinned, pointing the screen my way.

The message was from his brother: *Fuck off.*

Another text came in as I looked at it.

Don't crash it before I get to drive it, you lucky sonuvabitch.

Austin must've felt the vibration because he turned it around and his grin got even bigger. He didn't comment, though, leaning forward and resting his forearms on the wheel as he looked out at the people enjoying the night.

"Who's here?" he finally asked.

"Just...uhm. The—I invited the people from your old pack, the ones that stayed here after Kingsley visited and helped us that one time. And then a smattering of other shifters from the pack and from town. Kace gave me a list. I know he's your oldest friend here, so I figured he'd be a good resource. I didn't want to accidentally invite someone you can't stand."

"No gargoyles?"

"No. I...wanted you to be able to relax."

"Not even for protection?"

"I have you and your shifters. I'm protected."

He was quiet for a moment longer and my stomach clenched in unease.

"None of your crew?" he asked.

"No. Mr. Tom was very put out that I wouldn't allow him to cook. I had to give him something to do, so I told him he could come clean up afterward, but we'll be leaving by then. It's a Mr. Tom-free evening."

He drifted into quiet again, and I had no idea what was going on in his head. Had I screwed up? Kace had thought the BBQ was a great idea and long overdue. Although he and his friends had occasional get-togethers at each other's houses, no one had ever thought to invite Austin. I had a feeling, in addition to Austin being the alpha and always under a lot of pressure, it was because of me. They didn't want to welcome in my strange crew. They wanted to enjoy themselves within a close-knit circle of shifters, and Ivy House was not that.

"Look, we don't have to stay," I said into the quiet. "We can go. I kept all this super casual, so I'm sure no one will care if we take off—"

"It's perfect," he said, leaning back and reaching for my hand. "It's exactly what I needed. I can't... I don't..." He brought my hand up and kissed the tips of my fingers. "I knew I'd have fun tonight, regardless of what we did. Just hanging out with you is enough to guarantee I'll have a good time. But this..." He took a deep breath and looked out at the BBQ again. "This is exactly what I needed without me even knowing I needed it. The fact that you excluded your people..."

"I just thought it might be a bit more relaxing this way," I said in a small voice.

"It will be, baby. Thank you."

Smiling like a dope, I opened the door and climbed from the car. He took his time getting out, and in a moment I saw why.

"Bro," Kace said, sauntering up. He clapped Austin on the back, looking over the car. "New toy?"

"Look at this beauty," said someone else, a shifter I vaguely recognized from the bar. He wasn't officially in the pack, just living in the territory and working at a shop of some kind. "Good lord, alpha, this thing is sweet."

More people gathered around to check out the car. Austin left the doors open, describing how it drove and how fast it went. I might've felt a little bashful because it had a large price tag, but no one batted an eye.

After everyone who wanted a look got one, Austin closed down the doors and reached for me. People got out of the way, nodding and saying hi as he pulled me close.

"It's a gift from my mate," Austin finally said, heading toward the BBQ. "She spoils me."

"Not as much as you spoil me," I said as we stepped over a curb and into the park beyond the lot. The ground was covered in trampled-down grasses and springy weeds, not at all looked after.

"Hey, Alpha Steele!" One of the BBQers put up his spatula in salute. "We have all the meat you could possibly want. When Alpha Ironheart sets out to do a BBQ, she really does a BBQ."

Austin put his arm around my shoulders and walked me that way.

"Notice I just provided everything and walked away," I said as we neared, wrapping my arm around his waist. "I let someone else actually do the BBQing."

"This is a man's job," the guy said, and grunted like a caveman. "Ain't that right, Isabelle?" he shouted.

"I disagree with anything that man says," she called back from the fire. "On principle!"

A smattering of laughter went up.

The guy flipped a burger and then rolled a hot dog. Another shifter to his left poked a tri-tip with his tongs and still another, farther down, was working with chicken and steak.

"Go grab a plate." Mr. Spatula, whose face I knew but name I couldn't recall, pointed at the picnic tables covered in red plastic tablecloths and heaping with food. "There's plenty. Bonfire is...pretty self-explanatory, beer and drinks are in the coolers over there"—he pointed across the fire—"and there are plenty of chairs. Were you expecting more people?"

"No. The grocery shopper and setup crew probably got carried away," I said.

"Mr. Tom, right?" He nodded after I did. "That makes sense. Handy to have around, though. Once you're used to him fussing about everything, I mean. He seemed a little put-out that he had to leave."

"He wanted your job." I motioned at the grill in front of him.

"He couldn't handle my job." He winked at me.

"Thank—"

I cut myself off. Kace had instructed me not to go around thanking everyone for helping. By inviting them to a community event, I'd told them they were my community, and people in a community helped each other. He said I was doing plenty by supplying every-thing and organizing.

It felt wrong, inviting people to a BBQ, then having them do all the work. That's not really how it happened where I came from. I went with it, though. This was their culture. I'd respect it and be thankful I didn't have to grill.

"Welc—" He leaned toward me with a funny expression and glittering eyes before going back to his job. "Go eat. I'm starving just looking at you empty handed."

Austin nodded and led us toward the tables. "Mr. Tom must've thrown a fit about those tablecloths."

"Not just about the tablecloths, but about me

going out to get them. He gets really indignant when I do things for myself. Always has, since I first got to town."

"It takes away from his job."

"Then he shouldn't complain about the type of tablecloths I want."

He laughed softly as we reached the table. All manner of salads had been purchased—potato, pasta, and the kind that actually had lettuce leaves—in addition to buns, breads, cold cuts, and anything else someone might want at a BBQ. It was overkill but still low key, everything in plastic serving bowls with paper plates and napkins.

"Hey, alpha," a woman said as she grabbed a roll and a plate. "Alpha. How goes it?"

"Great, Marna. How are you?" Austin asked cordially, waiting for her to grab a couple of slices of steaming tri-tip with her fingers.

"Really good. Looking forward to heading back home in a few weeks and checking in with everyone."

"It's been a while. You need to take some time off."

She huffed a laugh, plopping a scoop of potato salad onto her plate. "You first, huh?"

She picked up a fork, those not plastic because I could not stand using crappy utensils when trying to cut meat, then raised her plate in a sort of salute and peeled away.

"This is you relaxed?" I whispered as I picked up a plate.

"I'm still the alpha. I can only fully relax when I'm

with family, and even then I can't cut loose the way gargoyles do. Or the basajaunak, for that matter."

"Yeah, none of them seem to care how they are perceived. Outside of professional hours, I mean."

"You know, I had a good time playing pool with Tristan a few days ago. After we got work talk out of the way, it was just...easy. Chill."

"He's got a good handle on his confidence, like someone else I know." He reached for a plate, but I held up the one I had. "I've got one for us."

It was his turn to pause, looking at it in confusion, and then me. A knowing gleam lit his eyes, and then a rush of heat filled the bonds. He pulled his hand away slowly, scooting in closer and using the other hand to grip my hip.

"What do you want?" I looked over our options.

"Why don't you let me do that." He took the plate and heaped on a spoonful of each salad. He balanced some bread on the side but left a large space for meat. After reaching down for my hand, he tugged me over to the BBQ.

"What are we looking for, alpha?" asked the guy doing the steaks. "Bloody, medium, burnt to hell?"

"Who would want it burnt to hell?" Austin asked. "Medium rare."

"There are a couple of people who have no taste." He smirked, about as much of an expression as anyone was making, and poked a few of the steaks before deciding on one. "Here you go."

"Thanks, Don. Need a beer?"

"Nope." He pointed to the side of the BBQ, where a Bud in a can was tucked into a beer koozie. "I've got one, thanks. Good to see you out and about. All work and no play makes Jack a very dull boy."

"I'll try to remember that when you're at home sleeping, hoping I've done a good job fortifying the territory."

"Don't gotta hope. I know it rightly. Enjoy."

Austin stopped by the drinks cooler. "Coke for me, Jess," he said.

"I can drive back if you want to drink."

"Are you trying to rob me of my fun?"

I fished out a soda for him and a water for myself, then followed him over to a high-backed wooden chair by the fire. People nodded and said hello as we passed. I expected him to grab the chair and move it closer to one of the groups of people hanging out and chatting. Or at least drag another over for me. He didn't do either —he just sat down with the plate of food.

"Uh..." I looked around, finding another empty chair on the other side of the bonfire.

"Here, Jess." He leaned back a little and put out his hands.

"Oh."

Feeling a little sheepish, I tried not to glance around as I took a seat on his lap. No one seemed to notice, though, or find it odd that a grown woman was going to sit on the lap of a grown man.

"Great," I said, and I knew I didn't sound totally comfortable.

Austin smiled in contentment, though, which eased my mind somewhat. I leaned against his chest.

"There's plenty of time for us to be alone," I said, "if you'd rather sit with the shifters. I have an afterparty planned. With just us."

His reply was silky. "I also have an afterparty planned. With just us."

"Right, but...maybe we should sit with your friends?"

He shook his head, situating me as he held the plate in one hand and the fork in the other.

"You clearly don't know how shifter BBQs work," he said.

I froze...I'd thought I'd gotten the info right. Kace had schooled me, after all.

His smile was not reassuring, though it was soft and intimate. He scooped a bit of potato salad onto the fork and reached it up to my mouth.

This part I'd been expecting. Shifter males had a strange desire to feed their mates. This behavior at something like a BBQ, in front of their people, was erotic for them. We'd done something similar on a smaller scale in the basajaunak territory. Kace hadn't mentioned the lap thing, but I could tell from the feelings through the bonds that it was heightening the feelings for Austin.

I wrapped my lips around the bite, leaning against him as I ate. He speared a bit for himself before laying down the fork and using his hands.

"I'm the alpha," he said as he picked up the steak.

Juices dribbled down his fingers, and I tried very hard not to grimace. "It's like a work function. I'm the C.E.O., and these are my employees. I mingle, friendly, but I must always remember my place. I'm their boss. I need to stay professional. We can make the rounds later. Let's just enjoy ourselves for now."

He ran the meat along my lips, and I opened for him, ripping off a bite.

His groan was audible. He watched my mouth as I chewed.

"I'd planned this because I thought you could relax here," I said after swallowing.

He fed me the next bit, his eyes deeply hooded.

"It is relaxing, knowing the rules, knowing what's expected. This is my upbringing, right here. It's comfortable."

"But it's not really an outing with friends. It's a boss with his underlings."

"It's an alpha with his pack."

I minutely shook my head as I rested my arm around his shoulders. "What would you do if I weren't here?"

"Visit with everyone. Engage in polite conversation. Eat, drink, be merry. Have a happier pack when I left."

"Excuse me for saying so, but isn't it a bit lonely if friendly BBQs or other parties are always work functions?"

He shrugged, feeding me more. "It's the job. But there's always the beta and family. Lines blur in some instances."

"And they don't mind if you give me all your focus?"

His smile was as soft as his eyes. "I've realized that shifters aren't so unlike gargoyles after all. Seeing us happy, together, advertises the stability of the pack. It'll give them more confidence in their leadership. In us. This is good, Jess. You did good."

I smiled at that, taking comfort in the knowledge that he always had me and Ivy House for more blurred lines. It was impossible to keep pretenses with my people. They were just too weird to make any sort of hard rules stick. I liked that about them.

"How's the situation at the fair?" he asked, taking a bite for himself.

I groaned and practically laid across his shoulder. "Sebastian and I had to go yesterday evening and reinforce the spell. Those flowers draw a huge crowd. They think they're computer-programmed and battery-powered. They marvel at the life-like effects."

"So the flowers haven't broken free and tried to kill anyone?"

"One tried, but Edgar was there to back up the older man trying to get a better look. He's been there twenty-four/seven, just like he promised. He skulks around at night, dodging the notice of the security guards, and sits there during the day, making everyone nervous. A few more days. It'll be over in a few more days, and then we can hack down those flowers. Hopefully."

He shook his head a little, the firelight flickering

across his handsome face. "What a mess. Is he sad that he didn't grab a trophy?"

I accepted some macaroni salad. "He won first place."

Austin leaned away, trying to see my expression. "Get out."

"Yeah." I laughed. "They gave out a few first place ribbons for different things. He got 'Most Ingenious.' Magical flowers for the win."

He chuckled softly. "There'll be no end to his joy at that. He'll want to go to all the flower shows he can find."

"Oh no. No way. He's cut off. I told him so, and I didn't even feel bad when he hung his head. Attack flowers at a fair? Like...come on."

Austin continued to feed me, his heart full and his mood buoyant. I couldn't help but feel bad, though. I'd wanted to give him a chance to be comfortable and relaxed with his friends, and he still couldn't do that. Not really. Maybe he could smile a little, or laugh, but only because he was in his mate's presence. That didn't seem like a good time to me. It seemed too formal for plastic tablecloths and paper plates. It was a steep price to pay for leadership.

Then I realized why his pack must've taken his car in stride. Why they'd marveled but not balked at the expensive purchase. He was playing at being down to earth, but was he really? His family had a ton of money. His brother had a car collection. Maybe alphas doing well solidified that image of stability within the pack. It meant the pack was doing well. And that gave people a feeling of security.

"Tell me what's on your mind, love," he said, and it was only because of his tone that I opened up and let it all spill out.

When I'd finished, he fed me the last bit of steak, his eyes locked on my lips as I sucked on his finger. He groaned softly.

"You're killing me," he whispered, and I smiled devilishly.

When everything on the plate was finished, he dropped it to the side, used his napkin to wipe off his hands and dab my face, and then pulled me in tighter.

"This is how it's always been done," he finally murmured. "Being an alpha comes with great responsibility. We put the pack above ourselves. Our family above ourselves. I'm comfortable with it because this is what I know, like I said. This is what I was born and trained to do. But I confess, I do like how loose and unrestricted the gargoyles are. I might slowly change the shifter dynamic in this pack to find a compromise."

I stood and then bent for the plate. When he tried to stand with me, I put up a finger.

"Let your mate look after you," I said.

He leaned back, his eyes gleaming, his gaze locked on mine.

I'd had lots of practice looking after a husband, but it had never felt this special. Maybe it was because Austin didn't expect it of me. Or maybe it was because he pampered me too, and I knew how special it made me feel. I wanted him to feel just as special. Regardless, I felt a happy buzz as I headed over to get sustenance for my mate. I felt a sort of peace I couldn't remember feeling before.

I got the meat first, deciding he needed tri-tip and also a hot dog. A little variety was the spice of life. At the picnic table, where before it was essentially just him and me, there were now a ton of people, chatting and grabbing food. It was clear they'd mostly stayed clear earlier to let us have first pick.

"Hey, alpha," a man said before a woman said, "How are you?"

"Hi," I replied, smiling at them, getting in line.

The crowd parted, waiting for me to go forward.

"Nope," I said, waving them on. "I'm not a shifter. It'll make me uncomfortable if I skip the line. Please." I waved them on again.

"But the alpha needs his—"

"You're wasting time," Kace said, walking up. He winked at me and directed a command at the others. "Stop gabbing and get your food!"

The nods and dancing eyes—the closest most shifters got to smiles—made me feel easier about the whole thing.

"You know," said Isabelle, a shifter I'd known since the beginning, "you make the alpha pair of this territory seem a lot more accessible."

"Probably a bad thing," I replied.

"When you're in his brother's territory? Almost certainly. Expect a lot of challenges." She gave me a poignant look. "And when you get those challenges, rock their worlds. Nearly kill them and then heal them, like you did with that enormous gargoyle you got working for you. For here?" She shrugged, waiting with me. "Here, I don't think it's such a bad idea at all. Those gargoyles are a bunch of..." Her jaw clenched. "They are a stubborn breed, that's for sure. When they stop being so stand-off-ish, though, they can be *fun*. And the basajaunak?" She almost fully smiled. "That one in the bar with the kilt is my favorite. Dave is great, but Kilt Guy is all kinds of a good time." She pushed my shoulder. "Listen to this: the other day a gargoyle was hitting on me. They're so laid-back about that kind of thing. I love it. I love that. But my ex, a shifter, got all bent out of shape. We haven't been broken up for long —the bastard cheated on me. Anyway, I was gearing up to back that ass down, but lo and behold..." She leaned away from me while giving me wide eyes. "Didn't that basajaun stand up, push through the crowd, and literally throw him out of the bar! He *threw* my ex out, ass over end!"

I gave her a funny look. "That sort of violence is against the rules."

She nodded. "Yes, it is. Except Alpha Steele was off duty and the beta wasn't in the bar, and absolutely *no one* was going to stand up to a basajaun. Not to mention that my ex deserved it and everyone knew it. When it was done, Niamh motioned for the basajaun to sit down, bought him a beer, and life continued on as normal. Zero residual drama. It. Was. *Awesome!*"

I didn't know whether to laugh or shake my head. "He's..."

"He's great, yeah. I like having the basajaunak in the territory. I like that they are here right now, watching our six from the trees. I tried to invite them to join us, but one of them said you wouldn't allow it."

"Wait..." I glanced around, running my gaze across the trees surrounding the park. I could feel Dave's location, back at Ivy House. He was the only one I had a bond with. "What do you mean here... *Here* here? Like right now, in *those* trees?"

Her grin was wider. "Yes. I felt them when I arrived, hanging out in the trees. Others have felt them, too, all around the park. They can hide really well but..." She gave me another comical look. "You can feel the danger when they're around, right?"

No. I couldn't. I had to actually send out magic, and I hadn't bothered. I should've, apparently. It seemed as though I just couldn't quit Ivy House—even for a single afternoon.

ELEVEN

Jessie

"Sorry." I looked back at the trees again. "I'll get rid of them."

"No, no." She motioned me forward to get food. "Don't. Like I said, I like them here. I had a great time at their feast in the basajaunak lands."

"It's supposed to be a shifter BBQ, though."

"Meh." She waved that away, waiting for me to finish grabbing Austin food. I noticed that everyone was giving me space. "No one cares."

Plate filled, I returned to Austin, now standing with Kace and Broken Sue.

"Hey," I said to Broken Sue. "You made it."

He inclined his head. "I wouldn't miss an opportunity to see the alpha's new sports car. That thing is a beauty."

"Isn't it something?" Austin asked, resuming his seat. "My mate is trying to shine up this old penny."

"Good luck," Broken Sue told me, his humor, as usual, not reaching his expression. "What do they say about old dogs?"

"Clearly something different than what they say about polar bears," Austin replied, reaching for me.

Kace and Broken Sue moved away, heading off to the drinks cooler.

"Was it something I said?" I murmured, sitting on his lap again.

"They're letting us finish eating."

"Crap, I forgot to grab a new fork."

"It's okay." Austin kept me from getting up. "Use your hands."

"But there's...potato salad and stuff. I can't use my hands for that."

His eyes were deep and open. He didn't repeat himself.

I did as he said, working with the meat first, knowing he was waiting for me to get to the rest. When I did, scooping it up with what had to be a deep grimace, his tongue swirled around my fingers as he sucked it off. I could feel his hardness against my legs and felt an answering heat.

"You're beautiful, Jess," he whispered before taking more. With me holding the plate, his hands were free to roam. They did so now, flowing around my hips and then one of them reached up to cup a breast through my dress. "When can we take this off?"

I ran my thumb along his lips before bending, capturing them with mine. Our kiss was sensual and slow, me only backing off because I wanted to get rid of the plate and just straddle him. I couldn't, though, not yet. Not until we got to the next thing.

"Later," I whispered, giving him more.

"Hopefully not much later."

"Don't rush your perfect night. Though I think it's falling apart a little. The basajaunak have apparently shown up. They are watching like creepers."

"I know. I felt them when we got here."

"And here I was saying that there was no protection but you guys. Why didn't you call me on it?"

He kissed me some more, and I nearly dropped the plate into his lap.

"Because I could tell you didn't know," he murmured against my lips. "You would've marched into the trees and shooed them away."

"I still will. I was just giving you a chance to eat first."

"No. Don't. They have BBQs like we do. Shifters in general seem to greatly enjoy them. Maybe invite them in?"

"Are you sure?"

He answered by nudging me off of his lap before taking the plate. He leaned down to grab the dirty fork.

"No, don't—" I snatched it away from him. "Don't use that. Gross. Wait there, I'll get you another."

He'd finished the hot dog by the time I'd gotten back and was working on the tri-tip with his fingers.

"Didn't enjoy me feeding you, huh?" I asked, handing over the fork.

"Greatly enjoyed it. I'm in agony from that enjoyment. I'm going to eat this, we're going to socialize for a little bit longer, and then I will be taking you home and getting to *later*."

I leaned down to kiss him before peeling away with a groan of frustration. I knew exactly how he felt.

A scan of magic revealed a dozen basajaunak loitering in the trees. I made my way to the closest—the first basandere who'd moved to my wood. She only revealed herself when I was standing right in front of her.

"Hello, miss," she said. I probably needed to assign them names just to keep them straight in my head.

"Hi. What are you guys doing here?"

"We heard you'd be all the way out here without any protection from your house crew. Given there've been shifter packs testing the territory limits lately, we decided we'd better keep watch over you."

"You walked all the way here?"

She looked around in confusion. "Of course. It's not far."

It was like ten miles from the house. Then again, Dave's mountain was much farther than that—and they were constantly coming and going from there.

"Got it. Well, this was supposed to just be a shifter party, and I don't want you to make a habit of crashing these types of things, but since you're here, please help yourself to the BBQ. We have plenty."

Her smile stretched wide. "Thank you, miss! It smells fantastic."

I held up a finger. "No fighting, though. No challenges. No getting drunk and rolling anyone through the fire."

"I'll make sure everyone knows, but there's no need for concern. We didn't bring any of our special brew. I doubt there is enough alcohol in those coolers to warrant any shenanigans, as Niamh would say."

Probably not, but you could never be too careful. It was important to set boundaries.

When I returned, Austin had just come back from disposing of his empty plate and soda can. He grabbed me around the waist and hauled me closer, bending to run his lips up the side of my neck before giving me a peck on the lips.

"And the gargoyles?" he asked, looking at the sky.

"Dang it," I grumbled, following his gaze.

He laughed softly, rocking us as he hugged me. "Just kidding," he said.

I continued looking skyward, though, and lo and behold, a large shape periodically deadened patches of stars. Checking in with my various gargoyle bonds, so many now they were hard to manage—I needed to work on that—I felt Tristan making lazy circles above us along with a handful of his people.

"I can't win," I murmured.

"It's fine. Mr. Tom was hiding in the trees on the date I took you on. This is a step up from that."

We stayed and chatted with everyone for a while.

The basajaunak made a surprisingly great addition—hanging out with the guys cooking the meat, lounging near the fire, and infiltrating the little clusters of chatting shifters. Their sense of tranquility outdoors relaxed the overall vibe of the BBQ, and soon a few of the shifters were actually smiling.

Broken Sue kept pace with us as we made our rounds, becoming my shadow and helping me with names. It didn't seem like he was interested in branching off, so I didn't shoo him away. Austin was polite and accommodating to everyone, rarely smiling and not laughing unless in response to something I said to him privately, but in obvious good spirits and happy to be amongst people he'd known most of his life.

After an hour or so of socializing, though, he couldn't keep his hands off me anymore. If he wasn't kissing me, he was holding me tightly, never letting me get too far away without reeling me back in. I let him call the shots, smiling as he excused us from a conversation and then told Kace and Broken Sue that we were going to take off. I said goodbye to the basajaunak and barely stopped myself from thanking everyone for coming.

"Thank you, Jess," Austin said as we reached the car. "That was exactly what I needed. I was feeling anxious about returning home, and tonight has made me excited instead."

"Good, I'm glad."

We got into the car, and after he started the engine, I said, "If it's okay, the night cap is at your house."

He paused, looking over at me. "Our house, Jess. Yours and mine. I haven't had a chance to talk to you about this, nor have I had a chance to get the paperwork drawn up, but mating is sharing a life. It's like marriage in the Jane world but more permanent. This bond between us—the way we feel each other—that's forever. It might seem like things haven't changed much because of my negligence, but when we mated—when your gargoyle finally accepted me—it changed *every-thing*. I want the house I built to be your home away from Ivy House, Jess. *Our* home away from Ivy House. And I want to make a more conscious effort to figure out how I fit into Ivy House. It helps now that Mimi is redecorating, but it needs to be my home as well. It's time for us to merge these two halves to create one whole, you and me. We'll sit on it for now, since we leave for Kingsley's territory in a couple of weeks, but when we get back, we'll sit down and hammer this out, okay? I promise."

I took his hand, my heart feeling like it was too big to fit in my chest. "Okay," I said, my eyes swimming.

"Okay," he replied, leaning over to kiss me. "Let's go home."

Austin

. . .

AUSTIN RESISTED the urge to stomp on the gas pedal in the new super car Jess had bought him. It was extravagant, over the top, glitzy, and absolutely perfect for an alpha of his caliber. At least an alpha of the caliber he was working toward. Kingsley's grudging jealousy was all the proof he'd needed.

The watch, though...

Kingsley didn't have the same passion for watches. He wouldn't appropriately *get it*. And Sebastian already knew about it, though Austin surmised he'd still be fine with discussing how fantastic it was. He wondered if Nessa had seen it yet. Hopefully not. He wanted *someone* to share in his excitement. Hell, he'd even consider showing Edgar, who would at least feign enthusiasm for Austin's benefit.

He'd taken a few selfies with it, a few with her, and a couple of her that she didn't know about. He couldn't help himself. She was so beautiful, such a perfect mate and leader. She had this way about her that made everyone feel comfortable. She'd been totally at home at the BBQ, ordering people around without meaning to. Making them go ahead of her or pushing the last cookie on someone. The ability to command showed an alpha's grit, but Jess's use of her authority to help those around her showed her goodwill and desire for a healthy pack. Most alphas strived to be like that, but he'd never seen anyone make it look so natural. So effortless. So absolutely genuine.

It would be easy to say the leadership came from her gargoyle, but he knew better. This was why the house had chosen her, because the female gargoyle needed to be a leader, and Jess had that natural ability.

Fuck, he loved this woman. She was perfection in pretty wrapping. He could've found no one better to lead with. No better mate.

He took Jess's hand as he drove slowly through the town, having taken the long way home. He was desperate to feel her body and taste every inch of her, but tonight had been so amazing. He didn't want it to end.

"I think you were destined to be a mage's mate," she said, her voice subdued in the quiet car. He hadn't switched on the radio.

"A mage's mate?"

"The mage side of a female gargoyle, at any rate."

"Why is that?"

"Because of the watch thing. You'll probably pick up how to read the subtle language of watches really easily. Broken Sue seemed completely at a loss when Nessa tried to explain it to us the other day."

He nodded, finally turning toward the house. "I suspect I probably will, though it sounds incredibly nuanced."

"It does. I wonder if some of that isn't just Sebastian reading more into it than other people. He's super smart. Surely the dumber mages can't read as many layers as him."

He laughed, once again resisting the urge to slam down on the pedal and feel the forward thrust of the car.

"He certainly does seem to think in riddles."

He parked out front and climbed out of the car, helping Jess out and walking with her to the porch, getting a last look at his gift as he did so.

"It really is spectacular," he finally said, unlocking the door and stepping aside so she could go in first.

"You should text a pic to Gerard from Khaavalor cairn. He'd probably call me up to curse me out for showing him up again."

She led them toward the kitchen but stopped just outside of it, her palms lifted to him.

"Okay, this is where I might just ruin your night," she said, and he could feel the unease through their bonds. "I needed access to your kitchen—"

"*Our* kitchen."

She paused, a shy smile curling her lips.

"Our kitchen," she said softly, a gush of warmth coming through the bonds. "Mr. Tom needed to set things up, but I couldn't tell you because I wanted it to be a surprise. Turns out, breaking into your house isn't very hard. Nessa found an open window on the second floor. We did a little B&E, but it was for a good cause."

He ran his hands up and down her arms. "This is what I was saying. I dropped the ball with the key situation, I'm sorry. I'll give you one before you leave, okay? I need to find a spare. I know I have them... somewhere..."

She sighed with a smile. "Okay, good. Night not ruined. Great news. Let's do the next thing."

"Is it later, yet?"

"Just about."

A fondue fountain sat in the middle of the island in the kitchen, spilling chocolate down its tiers. Beside it sat an empty platter. She went to the fridge and took out two baskets of fruit, strawberries in one and apples in the other. She set those down and pulled a cutting board from the cabinet.

"Oh!" She put up a finger, turning to the cupboards behind her. "Wait..." She put out her hands and froze in place. "What am I—oh yeah."

"Do you want help, Jess?" Austin moved around the island. "Do you need these chopped?"

"No, no." She pushed him away and pointed at the chairs. "Sit. I'll do everything. I'm not very organized in the kitchen, but I've got this."

Her smile was crooked and adorable. She grabbed a bottle from the end of the island and brought over two glasses.

"But you can open the wine, actually." She set everything he needed in front of him. "That would be a help."

She crossed to the little round table in the corner and returned with a plate of cookies and graham crackers.

The bottle of wine opened, he let her take it and pour two glasses. She lifted her glass and waited for him to do the same.

"To us. I love you. Thank you for making my life the best it could possibly be."

"I love you, too," he replied, clinking her glass and taking a sip.

"Mm. That's good," she said, setting her glass down a little too hard and then swearing under her breath. "Okay, so first..."

She pulled an apron from the hook on the side of the far cabinet before slipping off her shoes. Her eyes on him, she slowly pulled her dress from her shoulders. It cascaded down her body, revealing her bare breasts and lacy thong as it pooled at her ankles.

"What do you think?" she asked, slipping her fingers in the strap of the panties. "On or off?"

"Off," he said immediately.

Her smile was knowing as she slipped out of them, leaving them on her dress on the floor. She pulled the apron over her head, a little too big and giving him a peep show when she moved around. He suspected that was intentional.

"Come here, Jess," he said, painfully hard. "Let me touch you."

"Ah-ah." She shook her head, tying her apron. "Not yet."

Stalling in front of the cutting board, she pulled an apple from the basket and then pulled open drawers trying to find a knife. He didn't remind her that they were in a block right behind her. It was cute to see how flustered she got in the kitchen, as though any sense of order or organization just fell out of her head.

"Okay..." She paused for a sip of wine and then to

swipe her hand through the melted chocolate and suck on the end of her finger.

He started to get up, not able to take it, but she pointed at him.

"Nope." She quirked an eyebrow at him. "Be a good boy and stay there."

"Yes, miss," he replied, a shot of fire boiling his blood.

She turned, finally remembering about the knives, showing him her perfect butt. Back at the cutting board, she chopped the apples in rough, differently sized shapes before neatly placing them on the platter. Her belief that they'd actually eat any of this was delightful. He wanted to dip *her* in chocolate, not the fruit.

She went for the strawberries next, stopping to take a sip of wine. He watched her breasts randomly expose themselves as she worked, felt the glow inside of him that she was making him food. That she'd managed to knock this night out of the park.

"You dropped something," he said, pointing to a clean spot on the floor beside the island.

She paused, looking over the island to where he was pointing, then smiled a little as she got back to work.

"I noticed you haven't dropped anything," she replied, cutting the ends off a few more strawberries. "Or taken off anything. Or dipped anything in that chocolate for me to suck off."

He'd never lost his clothes so fast in his life.

She laughed as she pushed the platter across the island and then positioned it in front of the chair next to him. She moved around the island but shook her head when he tried to reach for her.

"Move back a little." She motioned.

"Please, Jess," he begged.

She didn't relent, exquisite torture. Standing in front of him, between his spread thighs, she reached back to dip a strawberry into the chocolate. With slow, deliberate movements, she licked the tip of it before biting into it sensuously. He groaned as she grabbed another and then slowly touched it to his lips.

She didn't go for a third, though. Retreating to the island, she put her hands on the edge and lifted herself up onto it before reaching back and undoing the apron strings. She threw it to the side and then brought up her feet, bracing them on each of his shoulders.

"Hungry?" she asked in a breathy voice, grabbing one of the apple slices and dipping it in chocolate. Her lips pressed around the fruit, transferring some of the chocolate to her skin.

He watched her in rapture, his hand rising and falling around his hard length. When she was done, she dipped her finger into the chocolate, her gaze rooted to his, full of fire. She dragged the chocolate-covered digit around one of her nipples before going back for more. Then around the second. She painted a little trail down the middle of her stomach before dabbing chocolate between her thighs, the area completely clean shaven.

"You wanted to taste?" she said, dropping her knees

a little wider. "Or would you prefer to dip and let me suck? The chocolate is a little hot, but it's nothing—"

He pushed between her thighs immediately, holding her knees as he licked the chocolate from her body. She dropped her head back, moaning, before running her finger through the chocolate waterfall again and sucking the contents off.

He rolled his tongue around the peak of first one breast and then the other, not wanting her to be sticky but not wanting to waste too much time there. He couldn't.

He took to her like a starving man, licking and sucking between her thighs before taking in the bundle of nerves and making her cry out in pleasure. He worked her with his fingers, too, the pace fast, almost frenzied. She gyrated into his face, fist in his hair.

"Mm, yes, baby," she said, a goddess on the kitchen counter, arching back.

He kept at it in the way she liked, taking her to bliss in the fastest way possible. She tensed, her breasts heaving. Then she cried out his name, shuddering against him.

He bent over her and wrapped an arm around her waist. Without effort, he pulled her to him and stood, walking quickly to the couch and laying her down. He was between her thighs in a flash, threading himself into her body in one hard motion.

She yelped and then moaned, clutching his body between her legs. He captured her lips while pounding into her. She reached between them, massaging herself as he thrust deeper and deeper. Her hips rolled, taking him higher, making him hit all the places she needed.

The climax came all of a sudden. He groaned as she shook against him, her moan caught by his kiss. She pulled her hand back and wrapped her arms around his neck, the kiss turning languid and content. He loved the way she acted just after being satisfied, her movements turning silky and her devotion to him cresting.

"Now we can try dipping and sucking," he murmured against her lips.

TWELVE

Jessie

I sat on the balcony outside of Austin's bedroom, sipping coffee in a bathrobe, looking out at the scarecrow trees of the coming winter.

Correction, *my* bedroom. He wanted to move me in! As much as I could be moved in, anyway.

I could see why he hadn't had time to sit down and hammer out the details. I couldn't leave Ivy House, since my protection and my people were there, and he'd go crazy if he had to stay there all the time. Maybe even most of the time. It would be a big adjustment, and I didn't fault him for dragging his feet.

But he wanted to spend forever with me! To share a house with me. To create a home.

How had this not hit me properly until now?

I'd known our bond was permanent and mating was forever, but something about the situation hadn't translated for me because of my Jane upbringing and way of thinking. Until last night, I hadn't properly realized the permanence of our situation.

Butterflies swarmed my belly. I wanted to show this new life off. I wanted to show *him* off.

I picked up my phone and took a selfie in the bathrobe and then a pic of the view. I added the caption, "View from the new house! We're moving in together!" with a heart emoji.

Then I hesitated. That felt a little presumptuous. What if Austin didn't want people to know just yet?

"Hey babe..." he said, leaning out.

His messy bedhead and glimmering cobalt eyes revved me up again. We'd been at it all night, only getting a little bit of sleep. I should've been well sated, but he was so hot with that deep voice, the muscular, cut chest and...

Well, I was easy to arouse, it seemed.

His eyes heated, reading me.

"Shower?" he asked. "Then we need to head out to the winery so you can give feedback on the tasting room."

"The winery... Like the real winery—oh, is this okay to post?" I showed him the would-be post, trying to squish my embarrassment over broadcasting something like that.

"The tasting room in the estate winery, not the

space downtown." He bent to read the post, and his eyes softened. "Of course it is. You don't need to ask."

I shrugged, sending it out into the world. "Old habits, as they say..." I crinkled my brow as I glanced at my account. There was a post from last night with a few pictures from the BBQ, namely the setup and a couple of Austin and me, one from a distance when he was feeding me a bite.

My face turned red, knowing I had non-magical friends and family that looked at this account. The lap sitting and feeding thing didn't really translate.

"Did you...send Nessa some pictures?" I asked.

"Yes. I noticed you weren't taking pictures, and she is going full steam ahead with Operation: Get Ex's Goat."

"Last night wasn't about him, it was about you. What about the one—this one." I showed him the feeding picture.

"Kace took that. I had him send it to her. It's my favorite."

Austin was tagged in the post, so I clicked over to his profile. My stomach might as well have dropped out.

He had a bunch of posts with pics from his life, which was great for his friends and family, but he also had outright braggy pictures, like of the new car and his watch. With them was the caption, "My baby outfits me like an alpha."

Alpha didn't translate much better than the lap sitting and eating situation, but showing all that wealth... No one from my old life would understand it. They'd probably think I'd turned into some sort of drug dealer or something. Or assume he was talking about a different girl.

Except he also had pics from the BBQ, all with flattering captions and cute sentiments. Then the last post he'd made, from just this morning, made everything explicitly clear.

It was a pic of me lying on his chest, the sheets pulled up just past my bust, something he'd probably done before snapping the image, and my eyes closed in sleep. My hair was fanned out around my face, dappled with sunshine, and part of his defined chest clearly showed. Only half of his face was in it, one of his beautiful blue eyes captured just right, with the caption, *This is what *forever* looks like.*

My heart swelled. I felt like I was living on a cloud. If I needed proof of the amazing man I loved, his account said it all. It was enough to end my thinking about my ex or my past life, even a little. It was the end of caring what others might think. I only cared about the present—and about him.

"Shower," I said, pushing to standing and following him into the house. He was about to get shown a lot of devotion for being so obviously my Prince Charming.

AN HOUR LATER, we rolled up to the winery about fifteen miles outside of town. Rows of grapes stretched out to either side and across the hills behind the small building. We owned all of these grapes and would use them to make wine, but we'd also buy from other vineyards for different varietals.

I felt Dave on his way, traveling by foot and likely bringing various basajaunak with him.

"Another big night last night, huh?" Ulric asked when I stepped out of Austin's new car. Jasper stood next to him, the two of them in front of a Town Car and apparently on bodyguard detail. Cyra and Hollace got out of the car, Cyra with a large smile on her face.

"What do you mean—" I cut off and gave him a long stare.

Austin walked by Ulric as though he hadn't heard, and Jasper put his hands up before bowing exaggeratedly.

"Would you guys stop?" I said, following Austin.

They fell in line.

"That guy is a machine," Jasper said. "I don't know about you, Ulric, but I am *incredibly* jealous. I think I have a bro crush. I want lessons. We have the same magic he does, but I do *not* have that kind of stamina. I've tried. Is it edging, Jessie, or is he knocking out some big Os and then going back for more?"

"I can't do either for that long," Ulric said. "If I tried edging all night I'd go crazy. I'd literally go insane. It would be a strange sort of torture, and I would love it as much as I hated it until I just—"

"Went crazy, yes, we get it," I told them. "We just love each other."

"That's more than love," Jasper replied. "He's got, like, a bionic dick or something."

I rolled my eyes as we entered the building through the wine-making area. Large stainless steel fermentation tanks lined the wall on one side and oak barrels were stacked opposite them, all the way down to the end.

"No Mr. Tom?" I asked as we met Austin at a service door and followed him through. "I thought he was supposed to come."

"He decided he'd better go check on Edgar, instead," Ulric replied. "We decided that was wise. Niamh is helping Phil with his brew in her backyard. Expect a messy drunken situation later. Nathaniel is training with Tristan, not far from here. As the gargoyle flies, I mean. He's on hand in case he's needed. Oh wow, this place is swank."

We walked down a hallway with arching ceilings and various racks for selling merchandise. We still needed to decide what to sell. I hadn't had the time to look into it. The space opened up to a large tasting room, with counter space on two sides and wine barrel tables oddly spaced on the main floor.

Austin ducked behind the counter, looking under the countertop and then turning around to check out the shelves, currently empty. Stone climbed to the high ceiling behind him and the floors and other woodwork were amazing.

"New tables," I said, wandering through. "A crystal chandelier or two. Maybe paired with old-school lighting fixtures. The kind with candles? But obviously not real candles."

Austin nodded and then stiffened, glancing out the window to his left. A large oak stood on that side, stretching out over lush green grass. Way beyond, picnic tables sat before the trees, mulch beneath them.

Wariness and aggression filled the bonds now, and Austin turned slowly to look at me, his eyes dark, his muscles flexed.

"What?" I asked. "What's the matter?"

"I'll check it out," Ulric said, quickly stripping.

"What's the matter?" I asked again, looking out the window.

Movement caught my eye, a shape flitting through the trunks and disappearing into foliage. A large wolf, obviously a shifter.

"It's not wise to attack when an alpha is with his mate," Austin said quietly, as though to himself. "He should know that."

Ulric ran in the opposite direction, probably heading for the cover of trees before he lifted into the air. He needn't have bothered. Another wolf appeared at the tree line, this one massive and stepping out like he owned the place.

"Summon Tristan for battle, Jess," Austin told me, his tone rough and ready. "This ends today."

"What exactly is *this*?" Hollace asked as we all started shedding our clothes.

"Can we kill them?" Cyra asked.

"Shifters have been attacking, trying out our

defenses," Austin explained as more wolves stepped from the trees. "We've been sending them on their way without too much damage, relaying the message that this territory is well established. They should've backed off. When they didn't, I wondered if the various attacks were orchestrated by the same group since they were all wolves. This is almost certainly my answer that yes, it is the same pack. Now here's the alpha, attacking when I'm with my mate, only a couple of pack members on hand for protection. He clearly hopes to take us down and claim the territory as a prize."

"He's an idiot," Hollace said with a laugh.

"That's a yes to killing them, right?" Cyra clarified. "It oughtta be."

"Yes, Cyra. This alpha has crossed a line in a big way. He's clearly asking to have his world ripped apart. I'm happy to oblige. Give them all you've got. Just leave one alive to tell the tale. I'm done with these attacks. Time to send a message the shifter world is going to hear. We're no longer just a pack. We're something much more robust than all that. We're something better."

More wolves stepped out, fanning out all around the building, standing close together. Far too many for us to combat alone. I'd forgotten to ask where Sebastian and Nessa were. They would've been helpful. But the gargoyles weren't far away. Neither was Dave, and he was coming fast now, probably having felt the shifters through the wood. Hopefully, he had some of his pals with him.

"Okay," I said, looking back the way we'd come. "Lock the doors after I leave. I can land on the roof. I'll call the gargoyles and have them sound the alarm. The shifters will get the message. We can stall until they get here."

"Don't bother," Austin replied, nude and fierce, going to the large sliding glass doors and pulling them wide. "I'm all the shifter we need."

Shivers coated my body as Cyra made an "oohh" sound, exaggeratedly shaking with a smile.

"Let's do this," I said, jogging out behind Austin and shifting quickly. I rose into the sky as my magic blasted out. *Call to arms! We're under attack!*

Wolves surrounded the property, obviously intending to lock us in. To trap and kill us.

Anger kindled within me, quickly burning hot.

Cyra flew into the sky in a jet of fire, but Hollace hesitated for a moment as Austin walked out a little ways and shifted. The great polar bear rose up, so much larger than their alpha wolf. So much more destructive. They had no idea what they'd gotten themselves into with him.

A familiar loud buzzing filled the sky. Tristan had gotten the message and started the territory-wide alarm. If someone couldn't feel my pulses of magic for whatever reason, they would hear the thrum of gargoyle wings.

Then thunder rolled across the clear blue sky, Hollace having shifted into his enormous thunderbird form and lifted up into the air.

The wolves tensed, one and all, looking upward. *Surprise!* We weren't an ordinary shifter pack, as Austin had said. We weren't an ordinary cairn, either. We were definitely more. *So much* more. They hadn't properly done their homework.

Austin roared, and I felt Nathanial and Tristan coming in fast. Dave, too, would arrive any second. Austin didn't wait, though. He rushed toward the alpha, covering a lot of ground very quickly.

The other alpha flinched, like he hadn't expected this to take off, and then he and his pack were rushing toward Austin, all at once.

My blasts of magic turned panicked, hurrying everyone along. Begging them to get there quickly.

Ulric and Jasper both dove, using claws to scrape across the backs of various shifters, while Cyra dive-bombed our attackers with fire. I flew to Austin as Hollace covered the other side of the property, his lightning raining down, his thunder filling the sky.

Austin reached their alpha and roared, swiping with one enormous paw. His six-inch long claws dug into the wolf's side, scraping away flesh and reaching the shoulder to break bone. The alpha yelped as Austin swiped with the other paw, ignoring two wolves that attacked on his right. I sent a blistering spell down to them as Austin's other hit took the wolf alpha in the head. Even as the wolf fell, Austin turned and lunged at the other wolves coming in strong. He swiped and bit, taking out enemy after enemy in a hurricane of violence.

I let him handle that group, sensing he had some aggression to take out, and worked on the would-be reinforcement wolves crossing the grass. My spells tore into them, ripping at fur and blasting sides. Lightning from Hollace and fire from Cyra did further damage. Ulric and Jasper were hovering low, fighting within the onslaught of enemy.

And then Tristan was diving into the fray from the treetops, having gotten there faster than the rest of our people. He snatched up two wolves, hovered in the air just out of reach, and smashed them together. They went limp and he tossed them away as the basajaunak exploded out of the trees.

Dave grabbed the nearest wolf by the hind legs. Before the wolf could bite, the basajaun lifted him up and then slapped him down, ending the struggle. He grabbed another by the head as the basandere from my wood snarled and ran past him, diving onto two wolves and wrestling them until they stopped moving.

Gargoyles flew over the trees, their attack formation perfect, trained by Tristan and currently led by Nathanial. They zeroed in on the enemies that weren't on fire, dead, or being attacked by the basajaunak. I flew above, ready to aim spells but finding no clear shot. Unlike when we usually did battle, we weren't outnumbered anymore, especially since Austin was working through the attacking pack like a comet barreling toward earth's total destruction.

So I selected one of the enemy shifters, a larger one with a burn mark on his hind flank, half an ear torn off, and limping badly. He was still in the fight, though, jumping up to try and get Jasper, filled with courage and led by stupidity.

He'd be the one to tell the tale, as Austin had wanted.

I wrapped him in a protective spell and grabbed and lifted him. The shifter snarled when I dropped him onto the roof. His nails scratched against the tiles as he ran to the side. He didn't go far, though, lowering down to his belly when he saw the drop. Instead he turned to face me, his lips pulling away from large canines.

I shifted into my human form so I could speak as Nathanial dropped down beside me. Good timing. If I got clumsy and did a swan dive off of this roof, he could grab me.

"You'll need to wait right—oops." I threw up a magical wall to stop the shifter from rushing me. "Nope, that won't work. I have magic, you see. Just stay put until Alpha Steele is through taking out your pack, and then I'm sure he would like to speak with you."

In no time at all, the winery had been cleared. Austin roared out his victory, anger and triumph ringing in the sound. He had a few scratches and bites but nothing that he couldn't easily heal himself. Still, I blocked out the pain for him.

The gargoyles rose high into the sky, beating their wings, chorusing Austin. The basajaunak joined in, and then Hollace and Cyra, everyone proclaiming their victory.

"Shift," I told the wolf, now eyeing me warily.

"Shift or he'll kill you." I pointed down at Austin, now looking up at us.

The wolf did as I said, turning into a brawny, brown-haired guy in serious need of landscaping his Netherlands. I put out my hands for Nathanial to grab and lift me.

"Tristan," I called, "take this shifter to Austin."

Tristan swooped in to grab the guy, then followed us down to where Austin had shifted into his human form.

Basajaunak checked all the downed enemy to make sure they weren't faking. Usually I'd try to curb such behavior, but this wasn't my gig. This battle was under Austin's leadership, and I'd respect his decisions.

"You'd wanted to save one."

Nathanial and I landed in front of Austin.

Tristan got within a few feet of the ground and let go. The man staggered toward Austin before he got his bearings. It was a nice touch.

Austin reached out for me, moving me so I was partially behind him. I knew it wasn't only for my safety—it was shifter language to show this shifter that I was his mate and he'd protect me with his life.

"Is your pack the one that's been attacking us these last couple of weeks?" Austin asked the shifter.

The shifter's jaw clenched. He didn't plan to answer.

Austin's face was granite. He shook his head slowly. "You don't want to play the silence game with this pack. We'll split your mind. It's a fate worse than death."

Austin's glance at Tristan was barely perceptible. Swirls of Tristan's nightmare magic washed over me, slithering along my skin. The shifter's chest rose and fell rapidly. More gargoyles flew in, this group likely coming from town. Shifters started to show up, too, running out of the trees.

"What is this?" the enemy asked through his teeth. "What unnatural magic does this pack possess?"

I couldn't help chuckling. He thought *this* was unnatural magic? Tristan wasn't laying it on very thick, and this was nothing compared to the power I could unleash with a similar sort of spell.

"This is the Dusky Ridge Convocation," Austin said, "not only housing our shifter pack, but the Ivy House heir and her crew. Your alpha didn't do his homework. Now, I will ask you one more time, and then I will let my mate consume you with magic. Has it been your pack—"

"Yes," the shifter ground out. "We'd heard rumors of magical creatures, but your territory is so new that my alpha presumed the stories were invented by your big brother to help keep your territory in one piece. We didn't encounter any of those magical creatures when we first attacked, so my alpha figured we'd guessed right."

Austin closed the distance and got right in his face. "Look at how many have died here today. *Look at them!*"

"I know how many have died," the shifter spat back. "They were my pack. You've killed them all."

"You surrounded me and endangered my mate, trying to take the pack like a bunch of cowards. You're *damn right* I killed them all. Let that be a lesson for anyone who tries again. Spread the word."

"To whom? There's no one left," he said, angry.

"To the next pack you slither to. Your people, those who lost family today and need somewhere to go, are welcome here. You are not. If I see you again, I'll kill you."

The man stared at Austin for one beat, just long enough for a rush of fire to light Austin up from the potential challenge, before dropping his gaze.

"Convocation?" he said. "That's what you're calling yourself?"

"We're greater than a shifter pack. We have some of the oldest magic in the world within our territory, some of the best and most powerful mages, along with gargoyle guardians and supernatural beings out of legend. What else would we call ourselves?"

He shook his head and spat to the side. "I'd heard stories about Kingsley's little brother before all this. No one thought they were true."

"And now you know different. Shift and make for the nearest territory crossing. You'll have gargoyles keeping track of you. They'll kill you if you stray. Got it?"

"Yeah," he grunted.

Austin looked at Tristan again, handing over the

reins, before turning. He kept his body between me and the retreating shifter, more silent shifter language that I didn't exactly understand. I'd have to ask him about it once things calmed down.

He walked me back into the winery, then picked up my clothes and handed them off.

"It's a waste," he finally said as we both got dressed. "Killing shifters is not what we should be doing."

Broken Sue ran into the area in his gorilla form. He must've driven because he didn't look sweaty or out of breath for running.

Austin paused before striding to the side door and pulling it open.

"Organize our shifters," he told Broken Sue. "Let's round up the bodies. We'll need to get them back home for a proper burial. Don't let the basajaunak get too extreme. If you can't back them off, let me know. Dave should know the drill, though. Tristan has the gargoyles under control."

Broken Sue grunted and got to work.

"Then why did you do it?" I asked, returning to our conversation. "I know you wanted to make a statement, but why did you go to such an extreme if you thought it was a waste?"

He shook his head. "They gave me no choice. Their pack crossed the line. They strategically tried to get us alone so they could kill us and take the pack. They knew the punishment for failure would be death. Any shifter would."

He finished fastening his clothes, shaking his head again.

"I want to unite them all, not take them out," he murmured, making sure I was ready before walking us toward the cars. "I'll tell Kingsley what happened, and he'll pass it on to the right people. I'm sure someone will check in with this guy or what remains of his pack. Word will spread. Hopefully, today's actions will be enough to ward off any other attacks until I have a chance to meet with prominent leaders. Obviously people need to see for themselves the power we've amassed and what we're hoping to do."

"Unite everyone?"

"Yes. I'll work on the shifters, and you'll continue to work on the gargoyles."

"We might need to send Gerard a car."

"It could help." He held the door for me and then handed me in.

"How would they have taken the pack, though?" I asked, trying to make sense of the thwarted attack. He started the car and pulled onto the road. "They still would have needed to get through Broken Sue. Then Kace. And all the other people who report to you. The pack wouldn't just honor that alpha's claim because he killed you, would they?"

"That alpha was incredibly ignorant." Austin gripped the wheel, driving too quickly. "He wouldn't have gotten through Brochan, no. Not a chance. Probably not even Kace, you're right. Our territory would've ripped them apart if they'd tried to take it. They assumed we were soft because we didn't kill them for trespassing sooner." He shook his head. "Idiots."

I put my hand on his thigh. "We'll bring everyone together, you'll see."

My phone rang and I glanced down at the screen.

"What is it?" Austin asked, catching the way I'd frozen in place.

"The ex. He's calling."

THIRTEEN

Jessie

Austin glanced over at me but didn't say anything.

I tapped the screen.

"Hey Matt, what's up?" I asked in a breezy tone.

"Jacinta, hello," came the familiar voice, always so formal. Once I'd thought him authoritative. Boy had that changed since meeting all manner of magical people, my mate and his family especially. "Do you have a second?"

"Uh...yeah. We're just driving."

He was quiet for a moment. "We?"

His tone annoyed me, like I was still his wife and had mentioned a guy friend. He'd never wanted me to be friends with men, even the dads from school who were happily married. Hell, he'd gotten weird when I went out with single female friends. Then, eventually, when I went out without him at all.

"What's up?" I asked again.

"It's been a while," he replied. "How have you been?"

Before I could answer, he kept talking.

"Jimmy said you looked well. You have a new job, is that right? A keeper of a house or something?"

Crap. I needed to come up with a job title to explain my sudden windfall to the people in my old life. Winning the lottery? A secret lottery no one knew about...

"I own the house now and manage its crew," I replied. "I'm doing really well, actually."

"You live in a small town somewhere...in the foothills, is that correct? Kind of a backwoods sort of place?"

I gritted my teeth with the condescension. "O'Briens, in the foothills of the Sierra Mountains. It's an up-and-coming town, but it's still small. And how about you? I heard you bought a new place?"

"Shortly after we parted ways, yes. In Culver City."

That was a part of Los Angeles that was trendy for young professionals or young families. I had no idea what he'd be doing there, given his dislike of young people and things they deemed trendy. Unless he planned on having more kids. His fiancé was ten years younger, so he might be gearing up to do it all again.

Thankfully, this call reminded me of one very

important thing—I did not actually care. Not even a little. My freakout from before had clearly been a case of temporary insanity. I wished this guy well and was happy to have moved on.

"Great," I replied. "Jimmy mentioned he was coming for the holidays, did he tell you?"

"He did. We're still trying to work out his schedule."

That meant that Jimmy had something in mind that Matt didn't agree with, likely spending the majority of his time with me.

"Well, keep me updated so I know what to expect."

"Sure. Listen, Jacinta..." He cleared his throat as Austin parked in front of our house.

Our house.

His and mine.

I smiled and looked over at him, seeing that he was watching me. I reached out for his hand, threading our fingers together.

"I wanted you to hear this from me directly," Matt said. "I've asked Camila to marry me."

He paused expectantly.

"Congratulations," I said, accidentally sounding a little bored.

"Thank you, yes. I want to make sure everything between you and me is amicable. Camila has some concerns. The right thing to do would be for you to come to my mother's Christmas party, as usual, and also attend our wedding so you can show your support of our joining families and our union. You need to put her at ease. With that in mind—"

"The right thing to do?" I asked, a little taken aback. "What does that mean?"

"I thought we agreed that we'd maintain a united front for Jimmy."

"Cordial parenting, yes, but we're not exactly friends, Matt. It's no longer my job to support you or your choices. It is certainly not my job to put your new wife at ease. You'll need to handle that. I'd rather not get involved. I have my own life to look after."

"Jacinta..." He did his famous huff, angry but too conditioned to show it. Instead he hid it in passive aggressiveness. "Why are you making this difficult?"

I sat forward, forgetting I still had my seatbelt on. It cut into me, yanking me to a stop. I hit the button to release myself before climbing out of the car, needing to pace.

"Matt, listen, you can invite me to the wedding. That's fine. I'll give you my boyfriend's name to add to the invitation. *Maybe* I'll go to the Christmas party if I am in the area and can fit it in. I'll certainly try to make it to both, but I can't make any promises. I have a lot going on here."

"We have months yet before Christmas and longer still before a wedding ceremony," he said. "Any plans you have can be moved to accommodate the events."

I stilled, just barely restraining myself from pulling the phone from my ear and throwing it into the trees. How had I ever dealt with this *me, me, me* attitude, with the condescension and the arrogance and the complete disregard for anything I was saying?

"And no, we will not need your...boyfriend's name," he continued, humor evident in his tone. It was always about tone with this guy. *Always.* "A simple plus one will be fine. We all know how fickle you can be, Jacinta, and how tumultuous you can make even the simplest of situations, as in this case. Not everyone is as patient as I am, and even then, didn't we find my limits?"

I stared at nothing in muted shock.

Had he really just blamed the failing of our marriage on me?

Had he seriously just painted himself as a saint for dealing with me all that time when *I* was the one who'd always bent over backwards to make sure he was happy? *I* was the one who had sacrificed my dreams and ambitions to create the nuclear family he'd always wanted. *He'd* always wanted, not me, with the dutiful wife who didn't anger him or speak too loudly or step out of her lane. I'd become the wife and mother he'd wanted, squishing the fire within me to do so, and in the end, he'd shrugged me off. He'd changed me to his liking, and I still hadn't been enough.

In times past, the command he'd just made would've crushed me. It would've brought all my insecurities raging to the surface, and I'd wonder if it really *was* my fault. If I was too hard to be around, too tumultuous, as he'd said, making life difficult for everyone.

Not this time. Not while still buzzing from battle.

If a woman sticking up for herself labeled her as tumultuous—as a problem—well, then...I was a fucking problem.

My hands started to shake. I struggled to control my anger.

"Did you seriously just say that to me, you ignorant prick?" I ground out.

The anger management wasn't rock solid, that was for sure.

"Jacinta." This time his tone was disapproving. "There is no reason to use that kind of language. I was simply looking out for your best interests. Your foul temper has gotten away from you again. I thought we'd eradicated that. It doesn't befit a lady of your stature."

I huffed in derision.

A lady of my stature.

He should hear what Niamh thought a lady was. What Ivy House did. It certainly wasn't someone who let assholes treat them like a doormat.

This is what he did, though. This was his playbook. He did something to anger or hurt me, or completely disregarded my wants and needs, and when I got upset about it, he played it off like it was my fault.

The dig about *stature* was a bonus. It was his way of reminding me that I was lower on the social ladder than he was. That I'd come from less, had less, *was* less.

Frustrated tears welled in my eyes. I wanted to throw the phone so badly my arm shook. Specifically, I wanted to throw it at him. Right between the eyes.

"Matt, let's get one thing clear. I don't care about

supporting you, or helping you. As I said—" He started to cut me off. "Don't you dare speak over me," I commanded, an edge to my voice. "As I said, I'll attend if I can make it work. But listen to me very carefully when I say this—"

The dead space was a little too dead. Years of experience had me pulling the phone away and looking at it. Home screen. He'd hung up on me, probably when I told him not to speak over me.

"That rotten bastard," I yelled, as loudly as I could. "He always did that. When I got assertive, or argued too loudly, or hell, didn't agree with him, he'd just leave the room. Or hang up the phone. Or refuse to speak to me until I'd *calmed down.* He is such an insufferable prick!"

I bellowed again, bending over with the strength of it.

When I was through, I wiped frustrated tears off of my face.

"Hey." Austin was there, pulling me into a tight hug and rubbing my back. "You aren't going to like this, but call him back tomorrow. Play nice. Apologize. Do whatever you have to do to secure that invitation."

"I really don't want to go to his mom's stuffy Christmas party so that I can be belittled or his stuffy wedding with his stuffy friends."

"Yes, you do, just to see how I handle his stuffy world." He pulled back, looking down on my face. "I've got you, baby girl. I don't care if it's a mage trying to kidnap you, a senile vampire trying to kill non-magical people with attack flowers, or an ex who needs to be put in his place, I've got your back. We handle things together. Get at least one of those invitations however you can, and let's see how he fares picking on someone he *thinks* is his own size." He leaned down to kiss me on the forehead. "Now let's go get in the hot tub and relax for the rest of the day. We've earned it."

He took my hand and led me into the house, and I knew what happiness really was. The Matts of the world didn't matter, not when I had an Austin. We'd brave whatever came together—first the threat to Kingsley, and now that I knew his game plan, maybe next I'd have to arrange a holiday gathering with the family, ex and all.

Tumultuous, indeed.

ABOUT THE AUTHOR

K.F. Breene is a *Wall Street Journal, USA Today, Washington Post, Amazon Most Sold,* and #1 Kindle Store bestselling author of paranormal romance, urban fantasy and fantasy novels. With millions of books sold, when she's not penning stories about magic and what goes bump in the night, she's sipping wine and planning shenanigans. She lives in Northern California with her husband, two children, weird dog, and out of work treadmill.

Contact info:
www.kfbreene.com
kfbreene@gmail.com

www.ingramcontent.com/pod-product-compliance
Lightning Source LLC
Chambersburg PA
CBHW021711190726
48289CB00008B/2481